The White Alley

By Carolyn Wells

Originally published in 1915

The White Alley

© 2011 Resurrected Press
www.ResurrectedPress.com

Published by Resurrected Press

This classic book was handcrafted by Resurrected Press. Resurrected Press is dedicated to bringing high quality classic books back to the readers who enjoy them. These are not scanned versions of the originals, but, rather, quality checked and edited books meant to be enjoyed!

Please visit ResurrectedPress.com to view our entire catalogue!

ISBN 13: 978-1-937022-29-7

Printed in the United States of America

OTHER RESURRECTED PRESS MYSTERIES

By Carolyn Wells
Raspberry Jam
The Man Who Fell Through the Earth
In The Onyx Lobby
Vicky Van

By Louis Tracy
The Strange Case of Mortimer Fenley
The Albert Gate Mystery
The Stowmarket Mystery

By J. S. Fletcher
The Orange-Yellow Diamond
The Middle Temple Murder

By A. A. Milne
The Red House Mystery

By Agatha Christie
The Mysterious Affair at Styles

By Arthur Griffiths
The Passenger from Calais
The Rome Express

From the Dr. John Thorndyke Series
By R. Austin Freeman
The Red Thumb Mark
The Eye of Osiris
The Mystery of 31 New Inn
John Thorndyke's Cases
The Cat's Eye

By Arthur J. Rees
The Hampstead Mystery
The Mystery of the Downs

Visit RessurectedPress.com to see our entire catalog.

FOREWORD

In 1911, when Carolyn Wells turned to writing mysteries, women authors were still the exception in the genre. With two prominent exceptions, the Baroness Orczy and the American Anna Katherine Green, detective fiction was the domain of men and the stories fell into two schools; the one, following the lead of Sir Arthur Conan Doyle featured cerebral sleuths who solved their cases based on obscure clues and deductive reasoning, and the other, primarily American, where the detective solved his cases with his gun and his fists. In either case, their was little room for character development.

Wells and her contemporary, Mary Roberts Rinehart, changed that by introducing a new style, distinctly American, and with a much more domestic focus. The characters and locales were based on the newly risen middle class of the eastern and New England cities and suburbs. These new mysteries were targeted at a feminine audience, and Wells in particular spent much time describing fashion and interior decor. The victims, and suspects, were as apt to be women as men.

The focus of Wells' novels was not with the details of the crime or the methods of detection, but was instead on the interaction of the various characters, their possible motivations and how they deal with the aftermath of the crime. Indeed, in the books involving the detective Fleming Stone, he rarely makes an appearance until the last few chapters where he comes in, makes a brief inspection of the crime scene, and then pronounces his solution based on a clue or two. It is the romances and jealousies of the possible suspects that consume the bulk of the books.

One theme that is repeated in most of novels is the domestic tension caused by the evolving roles of women in this period. The prime suspect is often a young woman who feels herself to be restricted, either by an old fashioned father or a domineering husband or fiancée. In *The White Alley* the question of whether marriage should be based on love or money is central to the story.

That this approach to the mystery genre was popular is attested to by the fact that in the thirty years during which Wells wrote mysteries she had over a hundred of the published. While on the surface, they may appear dated in their settings and manners, they address at their core issues that are still of interest today. It is with pleasure that Resurrected Press offers this new edition of Carolyn Wells' *The White Alley*.

About the Author

Carolyn Wells, June 18, 1862 March 26, 1942 was an American writer and poet. She was best known for her books of poetry and humor until around 1910 she read one of Anna Katherine Green's mysteries and took up the genre. Many of her mysteries featured the detective Fleming Stone. She was married to Hadwin Houghton, heir to the Houghton-Mifflin publishing company. She was a collector of poetry by other authors, and, upon her death, she bequeathed her collection of the works of Walt Witman to the Library of Congress.

Greg Fowlkes
Editor-In-Chief
Resurrected Press
www.ResurrectedPress.com

TABLE OF CONTENTS

CHAPTER 1: WHITE BIRCHES

ALMOST before the big motor-car stopped, the girl sprang out. Lap-robes flung aside, veils flying, gauntlets flapping, she was the incarnation of youth, gayety, and modernity.

"Oh, Justin," she cried, as she ran up the steps of the great portico, "we've had such a time! Two punctures and a blow-out! I thought we'd never get here!"

"There, there, Dorothy, don't be so—so precipitous. Let me greet your mother."

Dorothy Duncan pouted at the rebuke, but stood aside as Justin Arnold went forward to meet the older lady.

"Dear Mrs. Duncan," he said, "how do you do? Are you tired? Have you had a bothersome journey? Won't you sit here?"

Mrs. Duncan took the seat offered, and then Arnold turned to Dorothy. "Now it's your turn," he said, smiling at her. "I have to correct your manners when you insist on being so unobservant of the preferment due to your elders."

"Oh, Justin, don't use such long words! Are you glad to see me?"

Dorothy was unwinding yards of chiffon veiling from her head and neck, and was becoming hopelessly entangled in its coils; but her lovely, piquant face smiled out from the clouds of light blue gauze as front a summer sky.

Arnold observed her gravely. "Why do you jerk at that thing so?" he said. "You'll spoil the veil; and you're making no progress in removing it, if that's your purpose."

"Justin! You're so tiresome! Why don't you help me, instead of criticising? Oh, never mind, here's Mr. Chapin; he'll help me—won't you?" The azure-framed face turned appealingly to a man who had just come out of the house. No male human being could have refused that request, and perhaps Ernest Chapin was among those least inclined.

"Certainly," he said, and with a few deft and deferential touches he disentangled the fluttering folds, and was rewarded by a quick, lovely, flashing smile. Then the girl turned again to Arnold.

"Justin," she said, "why can't you learn to do such things? How can I go through life with a man who can't get my head out of a motor-veil?"

"Don't be foolish, Dorothy. I supposed you quite capable of adjusting your own toggery."

"And must I always do everything I am capable of doing? 'Deed I won't! By the way, Justin, you haven't kissed me yet."

She lifted her lovely, laughing face, and, a trifle awkwardly, Arnold bent and kissed the rose-leaf cheek.

Justin Arnold was one of those men whose keynote seemed to be restraint. Spontaneous motions were never his. Trifling, unmeant words he never spoke; and to imagine him jesting was impossible. Equally impossible to imagine him affectionate, or demonstrative. The kiss he gave his fiancée was formal but significant, like the seal on a legal document. It exasperated Dorothy, who was accustomed to have her very glances sought for, her words treasured and her smiles breathlessly awaited. To have a kiss almost ignored nearly took her off her feet!

"H'm," she said; "not very lover-like, but I suppose you're embarrassed at the audience." She flashed another smile at Ernest Chapin, and then said, "Come, Mother, let's go to our rooms and Oh, there's Leila Duane! Hello, girlie!"

Another motor came purring up, and a tall, graceful girl stepped out and joined the party on the veranda.

With a calm correctness of manner, she greeted her host, Justin Arnold, and acknowledged an introduction to his secretary, Ernest Chapin. Then, turning to Mrs. Duncan and Dorothy, she chatted gayly after the manner of reunited friends.

"How heavenly to be here for a house party! But I thought we'd never get in at those forbidding-looking gates. It's like a picnic in a Bastille or something! Don't you just love it!"

"I love it with a lot of people around," returned Dorothy, "but it is Bastille-ish,—in spots. However, as it's to be my life prison, I must get used to it."

"A prison, Dorothy," said Arnold, sternly, "you look on it like that?"

"Of course I do! But you will be a gentle jailer, won't you, Justin, and let me out once in a while to play by myself?"

"By yourself!" cried Leila; "imagine Dorothy Duncan playing by herself! You mean with half a dozen of your grovelling slaves!"

"Half a dozen or one, as the case may be, "and Dorothy laughed carelessly; "I'm not sure I don't prefer one to a half dozen."

Arnold looked annoyed at the conversation, but only said, lightly, "Of course you do; and as I'm the one, I'll attend to the half dozen."

"You'll have your hands full," said Leila, laughing; "are you sure, Mr. Arnold, you can keep our Dorothy in bonds? You know she is a super-flirt."

"Was, you mean," corrected Arnold, calmly; "Dorothy's flirting days are over."

Dorothy glanced at him, about to make a gay and saucy retort, but something in his face deterred her, and she contented herself with a side glance and smile at Ernest Chapin, which revealed small evidence of her subscription to Arnold's statement.

"Where is Miss Wadsworth?" she asked; "such a dear, quaint thing, Leila. You'll adore her! She's Justin's cousin, and, incidentally, his model. He's enough like her to be his own cousin! Where is she, Just?"

"She will see you at tea-time," he replied. "She begs you will excuse her until then."

Miss Duane nodded to her maid, who stood waiting, and, leading the ladies into the great hall, Arnold left them in charge of the housekeeper, who showed them to their rooms.

White Birches was one of the finest old places in America, and took its name from the trees which covered a large part of its one-hundred-acre estate. The house, built by the grand father of its present owner, was old-fashioned without being antique, but it lent itself readily to modern additions and improvements, and was entirely comfortable, if not strictly harmonious in design. Its original over-ornateness had been somewhat softened by time, and its heavy architecture and huge proportions gave it a dignity of its own. Justin Arnold had added many ells and wings during his occupancy, and the great spreading pile now possessed a multitude of rooms and apartments furnished in the magnificent style which had always represented the Arnold taste. North of New York City, on Washington Heights, it was scarcely near enough to the metropolis to be called a suburb; yet, easily accessible by steam, trolley, or motor-car, White Birches was a delightful home for its occupants, and most hospitable to the stranger within its gates.

"Within its gates is an appropriate phrase, for the only entrance to White Birches was an immense stone archway provided with heavy iron gates. The entire estate was enclosed by a high stone wall, on top of which was further protection from intruders by means of broken glass bottles embedded in cement.

This somewhat foreign feature gave a picturesque effect, and the old stone wall, built nearly a century before, was partly covered with trailing vines and tangled shrubbery. But it was intact and formed an effective barrier against burglars or other marauders. The great gates were locked every night with almost as much ceremony as the lord of an ancient castle would draw his portcullis, and though this excessive precaution was rather because of tradition than fear of present danger, Justin Arnold adhered wherever possible to the customs of his ancestors.

His grandfather, perhaps because of the other manners of his times, had an almost abnormal fear of burglars. His somewhat crude burglar-alarm had been replaced in later years by Justin's father, and this in turn by Justin himself, so that at present White Birches was fitted out with the most elaborate and efficacious burglar-alarm that had yet been invented. Every door and window, every cellar bulkhead and every opening of any sort, was protected by the tentacles of this far-reaching contrivance. The upper half of every window was further protected by a heavy wire screen or grating, which permitted the upper sash to be raised or lowered for ventilation without setting off the alarm. But when the alarm was set on, and this Justin Arnold attended to himself every night, no external door or window, with the exception noted, could be opened without the alarm being sounded all through the house, in the stables and the garage, where several men-servants slept, and in the gatekeeper's lodge.

The great iron gates were also connected with the alarm, and although the precaution seemed out of all proportion to the possible danger, it was a tradition in the house of Arnold, and was scrupulously observed.

Also there was a night watchman, who must needs punch his time-clocks at various stations in the grounds every half-hour.

There were telegraph and telephone wires, all laid in underground conduits, to prevent their being cut, and these gave quick communication to the police or the fire department in case of need. But though all this sounds complicated and ponderous, yet so complete and perfectly adjusted was the alarm, that the master of the house could turn it on in a moment just before retiring at night, and the butler could turn it off in the morning, and thus it troubled nobody.

White Birches could scarcely be called a cheerful place, for the grounds were densely wooded, the gardens broken up by ravines and rocky gorges, and the tangle of undergrowth in many parts so thick and dark that the whole effect was lacking in sunlight and cheer. But Dorothy Duncan had firmly made up her mind that when she was mistress there, as she would be soon, there would be a general clearing out on many of the acres. In determining this, she reckoned without her host and future husband; but Dorothy's was a sanguine nature, and she fully expected to wind Justin Arnold around her dainty little finger—although as yet the winding had made no progress.

As the guests followed Mrs. Garson, the housekeeper, upstairs, Dorothy paused and detained Arnold a moment.

"It's lovely of you," she said, smiling and dimpling at him, "to make this party for me. And I'm so glad I'm here first. I like to be first part of a party."

"You're the party of the first part," said Arnold, smiling at his own rather heavy attempt at wit.

"Oh, don't say that! It sounds so legal."

"Well, you don't want it to be illegal, do you?"

"Heavens, Justin! I didn't know you could even pronounce the word illegal! You are the ultra-quintessence of legality! There! isn't that a pretty speech?"

"No, it isn't, Dorothy, and you know it isn't. Why do you always make fun of me?"

The big, soft, dark eyes opened wide. "Why, Jus-tin Ar-nold! Make fun of you! I couldn't if I wanted to! Nobody could, not even Mark Twain, or Mr. Dooley, or— or a Roof Garden Man! You're not the stuff that fun is made on! You're a—a—"

"A what, Dorothy?"

But Dorothy Duncan knew and recognized that note in the man's voice that warned her she had gone far enough. "A dear" she whispered softly, and ran away upstairs.

Arnold brushed his hand across his forehead, as if to smooth off any perturbation that the interview might have left, and returned to the verandah to welcome other arriving guests.

The man was part and parcel of the old home. His fathers before him had stood on the porch, as coaches rolled up the long drive from the gate, and so he stood, to await the motors or station cabs that brought his house-party guests.

It was early fall. October, in merry mood, was gaily pelting the flying year with her red and gold leaves; showering them like confetti on a bride. White Birches was looking its best, or one of its bests, for the white of winter and the green of spring gave it different but no less beautiful coloring. But this season the leaves had chosen to turn superbly. No dead, rusty brown, but the whole range of the latter half of the spectrum, from gold to crimson and from orange to scarlet, rioted everywhere against the vivid blue sky. The great surrounding wall had all its prison-like grimness hidden by a blanket whose gorgeousness outrivalled a Navajo. Above it towered the tall old trees, that waved their branches with dignity rather than grace, as befitted the trees of the Arnold estate. And as its present master stood, looking with proud content at the majesty of his domain, he wondered for a moment if he had done wisely in choosing a wife to whom dignity and majesty were as nothing. To whom a gay chat, dance, or,—yes,— or flirtation summed up all that was worth living for. And then Dorothy's last words returned to his mind. "A dear,"—she had called him a dear,— and the thought thrilled Justin Arnold's not very susceptible pulses. After all, had his ancestors' wives been more beautiful, more adorable than the witch girl he had chosen? And, too, there returned his firm resolution that he had made before he had asked the girl to marry him,—he was going to make her over. Yes, his strong, firm, yet wise guidance would transform the witch girl into a calm, gracious woman, such as he remembered his mother and grandmother, and knew to-day in his Cousin Abby. Miss Abhy Wadsworth, a cousin of Justin Arnold's, was nominally the head of the house. Although a capable housekeeper and a complete corps of well-trained servants relieved her of all household cares, Miss Abby felt and enjoyed the responsibility of her position.

Of course she would soon have to abdicate in favor of Dorothy Duncan, but she was really glad that Justin was to be married at last. He was a man of forty years, and had grown so confirmed in his bachelorhood that Miss Abby had feared he would never succumb to any feminine charms. And then he had met Dorothy Duncan, lovely, bewitching, coquettish Dorothy, and he had immediately decided to marry her. He had no doubt as to her willingness, for was he not the wealthy Justin Arnold, master of White Birches, and scion of an aristocratic name and lineage? Nor had Miss Duncan hesitated. Slightly dazzled by the wonderful good fortune that had come to her, she had answered yes to his question, and now the wedding day was only a few weeks hence.

Dorothy was twenty-two and intensely romantic; but if it ever seemed to her that there was a discrepancy between her own age and that of her lover, or if she ever felt that Justin was a little lacking in his demonstrations of affection, she never shared her thoughts with anyone, and even her own mother had no reason to believe otherwise than that Dorothy was supremely happy.

But Miss Abby Wadsworth wondered. Not to Justin; it was not the habit of their family for the women to question or criticise the men's decisions.

But it was an uncertain outlook. Dorothy Duncan was too new, too modern, for the old-fashioned setting. Not so much the house, that had been remodelled and readjusted to suit other brides, but the customs and traditions had always been handed down as intact and as untarnished as the family plate or portraits. Ah, portraits! Dorothy would hold her own with those fair women in the picture gallery. Whatever Justin's bride might prove, she was a worthy chatelaine as to looks. And so Miss Abby's ponderings usually wound up with the reflection that Dorothy was a beauty, and, if she lacked dignity, she would surely acquire that as Justin's wife. However, Miss Abby knew the girl but slightly, and welcomed this house-party occasion to learn more of her.

CHAPTER 2: WILFUL DOROTHY

THE week-end party at White Birches was partly by way of an announcement, and partly because Dorothy had requested it. The girl loved social gayety, and to be the central figure of this merry occasion, yet without being the actual hostess of White Birches, appealed to her.

In the stately apartment assigned her, she was making a bewildering toilette, to do honor to her new position and also for sheer love of seeing herself in pretty clothes.

She had decided on a soft satin, whose quivering draperies of deep orange were veiled by a browner, thinner fabric, and whose velvet girdle was gathered into a buckle of tawny gold. From the half-low, rounded neck, her girl-throat rose in dimpled loveliness, and from the soft curves of her exquisite chin to the lightly waved mass of her dusky hair, her face was a sparkle of witching, tantalizing beauty. From a huge bowlful in her room she selected a spray of golden-rod, and thrust it in her sash. Then, with an approving nod at herself in the long mirror, she went sedately downstairs.

Dorothy was nothing if not dramatic. She had waited to make her appearance until all were gathered on the West Terrace for afternoon tea. Partially enclosed with glass, yet with wide-open casements framing the autumn landscapes, it was a most attractive setting for the gay groups gathered round the tea-tables.

Crossing the big living-room, Dorothy paused and stood in the open window-doors that gave on the terrace. Pensive, rather than smiling, she looked at the group a moment, and Arnold, seeing her, went toward her as a courtier to a queen.

Her hand in his, she stepped through the casement, and then, laughing, she dropped her dignified air, and ran to take her place in a large wooden swing, comfortably surrounded with scarlet cushions. One dainty, slippered foot touched the floor now and then as she kept the swing swaying, and, in gay mood, bandied repartee with the other young people. Leila Duane, the only other young girl present, was a complete foil for Dorothy. Leila's fair beauty, her golden hair and blue eyes and her pale blue crepe gown, set off vividly Dorothy's glowing type, her dark hair, her flashing brown eyes and rosy cheeks.

Two young men, Emory Gale and Campbell Crosby, partners of a law firm, and inseparable chums, sat near the girls and alternately teased and complimented them.

Ernest Chapin, Arnold's secretary, was also in the group. Chapin was looked upon quite as one of the family. He took care of Justin Arnold's financial interests, planned and advised concerning additions or improvements to the place, looked after the correspondence, and, moreover, was often of help to Miss Wadsworth in her social duties and responsibilities. Chapin was a clean-cut, goodlooking young fellow, though without the dash and fashionable nonchalance that characterized Gale and Crosby.

These two men lived in Philadelphia, and conducted their law business there. Incidentally, they were Justin Arnold's lawyers, and though he had little legal business to be attended to, it was a convenient pretext for them occasionally to visit White Birches.

Emory Gale was of a waggish type. He "jollied" everybody, he said impertinent things under the guise of innocent candor, and he was invariably good-natured and kind-hearted. But beneath his careless manner was a shrewd aptitude for business, and as the senior member of the firm he attended to the more important matters, letting Crosby do the routine work.

Campbell Crosby was a cousin of Justin Arnold.

Indeed, the two men were the only ones left of the main branch of the family, and, though several years younger, Crosby had always been intimate with his cousin, and the two had always been warm friends. As children, they had been much together, and Crosby had spent many happy summers at White Birches, admiring and adoring Arnold, as a small boy often does admire an older one.

The other guests were Mr. and Mrs. Fred Crane, he a naturalist devoted to his cause, and his wife a pretty little woman with sharp eyes and a sharp tongue, but whose brightness and vivacity made her an attractive guest. She was a distant cousin of Justin Arnold, and the Cranes were frequent visitors at White Birches.

But though all present were interesting or charming in their several ways, all were dominated by the presence of that most important personage, Miss Abby Wadsworth.

There are some women who possess the power of making their presence felt, and that without any apparent effort. Miss Wadsworth was one of these. She had only to sit in her accustomed easy-chair, and her very presence demanded and received recognition and respect. She was perhaps sixty years old, a cousin of Justin Arnold's father, and her manner gave the impression that to be a Wadsworth was far more important than to be an Arnold, or indeed any other name in any social register.

She did not wear the traditional black silk of the elderly cousin, but wore modern and fashionable gowns of becoming color and of modish though not extreme cut.

Everybody liked Miss Abby, and though occasionally she pronounced blunt truths, yet she had a good sense of humor, and was easy enough to get along with if allowed to dictate in all matters, whether they concerned her or not.

"You two men are inseparable," said Dorothy to Mr. Gale and Mr. Crosby. "I think I have never seen one of you without the other."

"You will, though," said Campbell Crosby.

"Just for that, I'm going to take you for a long walk around the grounds; and we may get lost in a wildwood tangle and never come back!"

"Like the babes in the wood," said Leila Duane."If you don't return soon, Mr. Gale and I will go out and cover you with autumn leaves."

"But you may not find us," said Crosby. "We may fall into a deep, dank tarn. I've no idea what a deep, dank tarn is, but I know there is one on the place. I remember I used to play around it when I was a boy."

"Well, I'd like to see it," said Dorothy, jumping out of her swing. "Come on, Mr. Crosby, and show it to me."

"Dorothy," interposed Justin Arnold, "stay where you are. Do you suppose I will let you go walking with another man?"

"Do you suppose," retorted Dorothy, "that I will ask your permission, if I choose to go?"

The lovely, laughing face was so merry that it took away all petulant spirit from the question, and Dorothy's dark eyes flashed with fun as she slowly went toward Crosby.

"If you want to see any part of the grounds of White Birches, I will escort you myself," went on Arnold.

"Oh, come, now, Justin," said Crosby, "don't begrudge me a little stroll with your girl. I'll bring her back safely."

"Let her go, Justin," dictated Cousin Abby.

"She'll enjoy a walk with Campbell, and goodness knows she'll see enough of you all the rest of her life! It's only a few weeks to the wedding day, and after that she can't go gadding about with young men. Run along, Dorothy, and flirt with Campbell all you've a mind to."

"Yes, do," said Crosby, but whether it was the too eager look in his eyes, or whether Dorothy suddenly decided to humor Justin, she refused to go.

"All right," said Crosby gayly; "but don't think I don't know why you refused. You just do it to pique me, and make me more crazy about you than ever!"

As all present were accustomed to Crosby's outspoken remarks, they paid little heed to this speech, but he murmured low in Dorothy's ear, "And that's really true, and you know it. And you'll take that walk with me, see if you don't!"

"Hold there, Campbell!" cried Justin. "Stop whispering to my girl! I declare, old man, if you don't let her alone, you and I will have to revive the good old fashion of duelling!"

"Oh, I wish you would!" exclaimed Dorothy, clapping her hands. "Leila, wouldn't you just love to see a real live duel?"

"Yes, if they all stayed alive afterward. But I shouldn't want any fatal effects; they're so troublesome and unpleasant."

"Take me away, Mr. Crosby," cried Dorothy;"I won't stay where people talk of such awful subjects!"

"Come along, then, and we'll look up that deep, dank tarn."

Dorothy rose from the swaying swing seat, and cast a slightly apprehensive glance at Arnold. But he chanced to have his back turned and did not see her. So with a beckoning smile at Crosby, she ran down the steps and out on to the lawn. Gaily she ran across the wide greensward and, rounding a clump of blue spruce trees, was lost to view of those on the terrace.

Crosby, following, found her there on a stone garden seat.

"You'll catch it!" he said, looking down at the laughing face.

"Why?" innocently; "can't I stroll round my own grounds, if I like? At least, they soon will be mine."

"Do you covet them so much, then?"

"Covet isn't a pretty word. Of course, I love White Birches. Though I never would stay here in winter. And of course I should want to go away in summer. But Justin says I may do whatever I wish."

"What portion of the year, then, will you spend in this old place you love so well?"

Campbell Crosby was talking at random, merely for the pleasure of looking down into the lovely face and watching the dimples come and go as the red lips parted. And he had his wish, for a slow, sweet smile curved the scarlet mouth as Dorothy answered:

"Only red and gold days in October; golden days— like—this—"

Her voice was low and almost caressing in its sweetness, her glance flashed to meet his, and then, with a divine blush, turned slowly away toward the fading sunset.

"Is this a golden day? Is it—now?"

The thrill went out of Dorothy's voice, the faint blush disappeared, but her dimples came into play, as, with a soft naturalness, she said, "Yes, indeed! Did you ever see one more so? The golden trees, the golden sunset, the very atmosphere is golden!"

"This hour is golden!" whispered Crosby; "you were good to give it to me!"

"I didn't give it to you! You stole it! Stole it from Justin, and he'll make you pay!"

"Suppose I make him pay? Pay ransom to get you back. I wonder at how much he'd value you."

"He wouldn't need to ransom me. I'd go back of my own accord."

"Not if I won't let you! Come, let us find the tarn, and then,—I don't know—I may throw you in."

"What is a tarn, really?" and Dorothy rose and walked with Crosby toward the ravines.

Only about an acre of White Birches was lawn.

Once off that, the grounds became almost like woodland. There were brooks, tiny falls, hillocks, and sometimes deep undergrowth. Much had been made by clever landscape gardeners, but, wherever possible, the old natural beauties were there. Dorothy had seen little of it all. One brief, previous visit had shown her only the gardens and lawns near the house.

She said as much to Crosby, and he replied:"Then old Just will give it to me, for sure!"

"Let's go back," said Dorothy, frightened as they found themselves farther and farther from the house.

But Crosby walked slowly on, and answered her earlier remark.

"Don't you know what a tarn is? Don't you remember Tennyson's line, 'a glen, gray bowlder and black tarn '?"

"No, but it sounds like Hallowe'en! Is it?"

Crosby laughed out. "You kiddy! Is that what that line makes you think of? By Jove I wish it were Hallowe'en! Maybe I wouldn't try my fate with you!"

"You couldn't; my fate is settled. But I'm going to make Justin let me have a Hallowe'en party! Won't it be fun! Now, show me the tarn."

"That's it,—before you."

"Why, that's only a pool of water! Not clear water, at that."

"But that's all a tarn is,—a pool of water. But if it's deep and black and generally shuddery-looking, it can be called a tarn."

"Well, I don't think much of your old tarn. Come on, let's go back."

"I know why. Because the sun has almost set, and the air is cool and this place is gloomy, and so,— it makes you begin to think of how Justin will scold you!"

Crosby's voice was almost triumphant, and Dorothy looked at him in surprise.

"Why, one would think you were glad I'm to be scolded!"

"I am."

"You are! Why?"

"Because you are to be scolded for having run away with me. With me!" Crosby added, exultantly. "I'd be glad to have you often scolded for that!"

Dorothy turned and flashed her dark eyes at him.

"Do you suppose for a minute that Justin will really scold me? Indeed, he won't! Nobody scolds me unless I choose to be scolded! If he tries it, I shall smile at him. You can't scold a smiling person, can you?"

Apparently Justin Arnold couldn't, for within five minutes of the runaways' return, Dorothy was nestled into a cushioned settee, and her fiance was striving to please her somewhat capricious appetite for "icy cakes,— the creamy-inside kind."

Chapter 3: May and December

"I WISH I were three people!" exclaimed Leila Duane; "I want to walk and motor and play golf all at once"

It was after luncheon the next day, and the house-party congregated for a moment on the terrace, before breaking up into smaller groups. The air was full of that October warmth, so much more life-giving and blood-stirring than even the early days of spring.

"It's utterly absurd, Dorothy," said Mabel Crane, "for you to think of getting married! You look about fourteen to-day!"

Dorothy was in walking rig of greenish tweeds. She wore a white silk blouse with a scarlet tie and a soft green felt hat with scarlet quill. Her skirt was ankle length and her low russet shoes showed a glimpse of scarlet stockings.

"I'm going to be fourteen as long as I can," she returned, smiling; "soon enough I shall have to become Justin's age,—what is it, Just? Sixty?"

"No, he's only forty," put in Miss Abby, seriously; "and you mustn't tease him about it, Dorothy."

"Oh, is he sensitive?" and Dorothy pretended to be embarrassed. "Why, I'm sure you look quite youthful, dear." And going to Arnold's side, she laid her hand on his shoulder, and scrutinized his face. The contrast was marked. Though a fairly handsome man, Justin Arnold looked his full age, and his stern, set face looked old indeed, beside Dorothy's laughing dimples and shining eyes. "And anyway, when we're married, I think I won't become Justin's age,—but make him become mine. How'd you like to be twenty-two, Justy?"

"I'll be in my second childhood, if you say so," returned Arnold, and Dorothy rewarded him for this pretty speech with a little tweak of his graying hair.

"You seem to know how to manage him, all right," laughed Mrs. Crane, "so I suppose you are old enough to be married, after all. What are you going to wear at your wedding? A short skirt and TamO'Shanter?"

"White, I suppose; but I do think it's awfully hackneyed! I wish I could wear some bright color."

"Why, Dorothy, how you talk," exclaimed her mother, who was always shocked at the slightest unconventionality.

"She's right," said Emory Gale; "one does get awfully tired of a white-robed bride. Now a lot of gay colors,— Scotch plaid for choice,—would be awfully fetching."

"How foolish men are," said Mrs. Crane, with an air of saying something new; "of course your gown'll be white, Dorothy; ivory satin, I suppose, with an embroidered train, and a priceless lace veil."

"I suppose so," said Dorothy, with a resigned air. "I say, Justin, if I've got to have that wedding dress, and so soon, can't I run away and play with Campbell just a little while? He has asked me to."

"Yes, go," said Arnold, frowning; "go and stay as long as you like! What do I care?"

"Come on, then," said Dorothy, tucking her through Crosby's arm.

But now, perhaps because of his cousin's frown, Crosby did not seem so anxious for the walk. "I was only fooling," he said.

"But I wasn't," persisted Dorothy; "well, if you won't go, who will accompany me for a little stroll?"

Three men started toward her at once. Arnold himself was the first one; Emory Gale stepped forward, smiling; and with a slightly hesitating step, Ernest Chapin came toward Dorothy and bowed gravely.

"Why, Mr. Chapin," cried the little coquette, "I'd rather stroll with you than anybody. Come on."

The two walked away, and Arnold's brow cleared. He was quite willing Dorothy should walk with his quiet-mannered and rather dull secretary, but he did not want her to go frisking about with gay young men of her own set.

"She's a case," said Mrs. Crane to Miss Wadsworth, as they watched the pair depart.

"A very sweet dear little case," returned Miss Abby, fairly bristling in defence of Dorothy.

"She's so pretty and attractive, she can't help being a little coquettish; but she really does it to tease old Justin, and it does him good, too. He's forty years old and she's only twenty-two. That's too much difference altogether; but Dorothy knows what she's about, and she'll make that man younger by many years with her pretty frivolities."

"I think it a little dangerous," said Mrs. Crane, who rarely hesitated to say what she thought.

"Dangerous? How do you mean?" said Dorothy's mother, and the gleam that came into her eye was markedly dangerous of itself.

Mrs. Crane quailed before it. "I didn't mean anything much," she said, "but eighteen years is a big difference in age between husband and wife. But I'm sure I hope they'll be happy."

"Of course they'll be happy," said Mrs. Duncan.

"Mr. Arnold is of a kind and lovable disposition. He's a true gentleman, and he is generous and wise."

"He's a crank, that's what he is," said Miss Wads worth, with an air of settling the question; "a man can't be a bachelor of forty, without having cranky ways, and as I know him pretty well, I know he isn't very easy to get along with. But Dorothy can tame him, if anybody can, and she's going about it just the right way. A patient Griselda couldn't do anything with Justin, but a little witch like Dorothy can rule him with a flash of her bright eye."

"Yes," said Mrs. Duncan, complacently, "that's what I think."

"But does she love him?" persisted Mrs. Crane, who never knew when to stop asking questions.

"My daughter wouldn't marry a man she didn't love," and Mrs. Duncan put on a superior air that silenced though it didn't convince Mabel Crane.

"Of course," said Miss Abby, "Dorothy loves Justin, and it's a fine match for her from every point of view. A kind husband with lots of money, and a beautiful big home like this, is better for any girl than a foolish romance with some young whippersnapper, with nothing but poverty to look forward to."

This speech seemed to require no answer, and Mrs. Duncan smoothed the silken folds of her gown complacently, while Mrs. Crane let her pretty face assume a cynical expression.

"If Justin didn't marry," Mrs. Crane asked, "what would eventually become of the property?"

"Campbell Crosby is really the next heir," said Miss Abby, "though he belongs to a different branch of the family."

"But yourself?" went on Mrs. Crane, with some curiosity; "wasn't your mother an Arnold?"

"Yes; but of course I wouldn't be the heir. Justin has made a will, leaving me a big legacy, but except for that, and a few other legacies, his whole estate, including White Birches, would go to Campbell."

"Campbell Crosby seems out of place in a home like this," commented Mrs. Duncan; "it just suits Justin Arnold to be at the head of a big country house, but that feather-brained young fellow seems better adapted to city life."

"Yes, he always lives in a hotel in Philadelphia," said Miss Abby. "Nothing would induce him, he has often said, to live the life of a country gentleman. Many a time I've heard him tell Justin he didn't see how any man could stand it to be mewed up inside these stone walls; though he likes well enough to run down here for an occasional week-end.But when he was a boy, he used to be here for months at a time. He liked it then, well enough. Though eight years younger than Justin, they were good comrades, and wherever Justin would go, Campbell would follow. My! I've seen them climbing sloping turret roofs, and walking around the tower battlements till it fairly made my hair stand on end. They were harum-scarum boys. And Campbell is that still, though Justin quieted down as he grew older."

"Yes, Justin seems very staid," said Mabel Crane, "though I dare say his marriage to a bright young thing like Dorothy will have a rejuvenating effect on him."

"I dare say," said Miss Abby, drily, "and of course it cuts Campbell out of the inheritance. I've no doubt Justin will leave him a handsome legacy in his will, but of course Dorothy will be his heir."

"My ears burn," said Crosby, walking toward the group of chatting ladies; "Miss Duane has gone off skylarking with Gale, and, being left alone, I tried to listen to what you fair ladies might be saying, and was rewarded by hearing my own name."

"Yes," said Miss Abby, smiling at the pleasant face of the young man, "we were saying that Justin's marriage will cut off your hopes of inheriting his estate."

Crosby gave her a slightly reproachful glance."Dear Miss Abby," he said, "I don't think I've ever given you reason to talk like that. I've never looked upon myself as heir to White Birches, and I wouldn't want it anyway, though I don't mean that for 'sour grapes.' I hope old Just will live heaps of years yet to enjoy it, and Dorothy, too." His voice broke a little as he mentioned the girl's name, and, as his hearers were well aware of his feeling toward her, they quite understood.

Just then Arnold came by and paused to listen.

"No, old Just," and Crosby turned to his cousin, "I don't want your fortune and I don't want this feudal castle of yours, but unless you're pretty careful, I'll kidnap your girl and carry her off."

"You can't do it, Cam," and Arnold put his hand on the other man's shoulder; "not only is Dad's old burglar alarm in good working order, but I've added some modern contraptions, that make it impossible for anyone to get in or out of White Birches unbeknownst."

"Love laughs at locksmiths," said Campbell, saucily; and Mrs. Duncan observed, "And then, too, Mr. Crosby, you'd have to get Dorothy's consent first; I hardly think she'd be willing to be kidnapped."

"Oh, kidnappers never ask permission of their victims," retorted Crosby; "I should spirit her away without anyone knowing it."

Arnold looked at the speaker a little quizzically.

"Then why didn't you go to walk with her this afternoon?" he said.

Crosby looked him straight in the eye, and said, quietly, "Because you didn't want me to."

"Good old man!" and Arnold's tone and expression betrayed the real feeling he felt for this manly behavior.

"But I mightn't always be so punctilious," laughed Crosby, who. was determined not to treat the matter seriously; "another time I may take her to walk, whether with your permission or without it."

"I'll trust you, old man." And this was corroborated by a hearty slap on the shoulder. "By the way, Cam, I wish you'd come for a stroll with me; I want to talk over some business matters."

Rightly guessing that it was in regard to the making of a new will, Crosby sauntered off with his cousin.

"You see," Arnold said, "if I didn't marry, old chap, my fortune would fall to your share eventually."

"Fiddlesticks!" returned his cousin. "Any one would think you were, a doddering old gentleman, and I your young and upstart heir. Please remember I'm only eight years younger than you are, so I hold we're contemporaries, and have little chance of inheriting from

each other. And, any way, Just, I wish you'd cut out that
kind of talk. You know perfectly well I don't want your
riches nor this fortified old barracks of yours, either. But
I do wish you hadn't selected for your future bride the
only girl I ever loved."

"The latest, you mean," said Arnold, slightly smiling.
"I remember definitely about a score of those 'only girls
you ever loved,' and I think there are a few I've
forgotten."

"Oh, come now, I never really loved anyone but
Dorothy."

"I'm truly sorry, old chap, but it can't be helped now.
And I'd feel sorrier still, but that I know you'll find
another only girl to love, now that Dorothy is out of the
running. And now, Cam, I want you and Gale to draw me
up a new will. I'm going to leave a fairish little sum to
you, whether you want it or not; and a bunch to Cousin
Abby, and a good bit to Driggs and Peters."

"And the housekeeper?"

"Oh, yes, Mrs. Carson. But these legacies are the
same as they stand in my present will."

"Oh, cut it, Justin! You're only making this will
because you think it devolves on the head of the house of
Arnold to do that sort of thing. Don't bother about it for
the present. You'll be married in a few weeks, and then
Dorothy will be your legal heir, and you can fix up your
will and that precious legacy to me afterwards."

"You're a good sort, Campbell. I have got a lot of
things to attend to before the wedding, so perhaps it
would be as well to leave that matter until afterward.
Anyway, I suppose I'd better take up the subject with
Gale. It might be less embarrassing, as I'm not going to
leave him anything. Or, if you prefer, I'll get another
lawyer for the purpose."

"Do as you like, old chap; but I say, Just, I wish you'd
let me off from being your best man. Truly, I'm hard hit
by that little black-eyed witch, and, confound it! a fellow

hates to stand tamely by and fairly assist another fellow to marry the girl he cares for!"

"Why, Cam, I didn't know you were so serious as all that. Of course, I'll let you off, if you insist. Chapin could be my best man, I suppose—or Gale— or even Fred Crane. There are plenty of fellows, but I expected to have you."

"Well, I'd rather you'd get someone else, if you will. I say, Justin, do you remember the day we climbed that turret? Shinned up the outside! We were a venturesome pair of kids, weren't we?"

"Yes; I expect there were mighty few places about this old house that we didn't climb up or over or through."

"And you used to boost me up into all sorts of dark holes where you were too big to get in yourself, and I felt honored to be used for such a purpose! We never climbed over the wall, did we?"

"No, we never could manage that. That's a pretty good wall, Cam."

"Yes, as walls go. But I think it's a blot on the landscape. It's of no earthly use; why don't you tear it down?"

"Tear it down! I'd as soon think of razing the house to the ground! It's a stunning old pile, isn't it?"

The two men stood on a knoll which gave one of the best views of the old mansion. The additions that had been made from time to time were not inharmonious, and though it was a rambling structure it was as a whole pleasing to the eye.

"I shall make quite a lot of changes for Dorothy," Justin said; "I think I'll put up a whole new wing, and let her have a suite of rooms with every possible modern beauty of decoration and appointment."

"Do! You're a lucky dog, Just, to have the privilege of doing things for that girl. Oh, well, it's all in a lifetime!"

The two men walked on in silence for a few minutes, and then as by a common impulse, they turned and went back to the house to join the others.

But as everybody was dressing for dinner, the terrace was deserted.

"There's a dance on to-night, old man," said Arnold;" just a small one, but Dorothy wanted some amusement, so I invited a few of the neighbors."

"All right," answered Crosby, and he went on to the smoking-room.

CHAPTER 4: WITH DANCING STEPS

DINNER that night was a gay function. A few of the dance guests had been invited to dine and more would come later.

Dorothy appeared in a daring little dancing frock of scarlet chiffon, whose low bodice showed her girlish, dimpled shoulders and rounded, baby-like arms. She was quite in her element, for by virtue of her position she was queen of the occasion, and by virtue of her charms and fascination she was easily belle of the ball.

Leila, in pale green, was beautiful, but her exquisite blonde beauty faded and paled beside Dorothy's sparkling witchery.

Mrs. Duncan, shining in the reflected light of her daughter, was calmly gracious of manner, and in her white silk clouded with black lace looked charmingly attractive.

But far from being outshone by her younger guests, Miss Wadsworth appeared in the full glory of a rose-colored satin, with much point lace and many jewels.

"Don't come near me, child," she cried, as she saw Dorothy's scarlet frills. "Why didn't you let me know you were going to wear red? Never mind; keep the length of the room between us for this evening, and hereafter we'll compare notes before we dress."

Dorothy laughed, and promised to stay away from Miss Wadsworth, and keep near Mrs. Crane, who in pale corn-color harmonized with Dorothy's brilliant garb.

But the red frock was not often seen beside the yellow one, for Dorothy was beset on all sides by would-be partners. Her dances were divided, and the intervals between them were carefully portioned out to eager swains, some of whom met the little witch for the first time that evening.

"Isn't this my dance?" said Arnold, coming up to her as she sat in a window-seat with Emory Gale.

"I hope so," said Gale, "for perhaps you'll be able to keep this young person in order. She's flirting desperately all over the place, and has even tried her beguiling arts on me."

"Nothing of the sort," said Dorothy, pouting.

"I shouldn't waste them on you—you're too unappreciative!" Then, turning to Arnold, with an exaggerated gesture of appeal, she said, "Let me fly with you, oh lord of my life! Every one else bores me to extinction, and I live only in hope of being again with you!"

Though these fervid words were uttered in deep, vibrant tones, Dorothy's glances strayed wickedly toward Gale, and the humorous twinkle in her eyes proved that her speech was merely a joke born of her high spirits and love of foolery.

But Arnold grasped her arm and drew her almost roughly out of the dancing-room, through the great hall, and out on a small veranda, where they found themselves alone in the moonlight.

"Dorothy," he exclaimed, in angry accents, "what do you mean by guying me like that? Don't you know I won't stand it?"

"I know you will," cooed Dorothy, as with her little finger-tips she daintily patted his bronzed cheek.

The touch of those soft fingers put an end to scolding, as Dorothy knew it would, but though Justin's arm went round her, and his voice became tender and lover-like, he could not resist a little more plain speaking.

"It's bad enough now, when we're only engaged, but if after we're married you go flirting about with every Tom, Dick, and Harry, there'll be trouble."

"There'll be trouble, anyway, after I'm married—;" and Dorothy drew down the corners of her dimpled mouth with the expression of one who foresees dire disaster.

"What do you mean by that?"

"Oh, Justin, you're so severe and hard and dictatorial! I just know you won't let me do anything after we're married!"

"Then, why do you marry me?"

"Because I want to. But I do want you to be a little kinder to me, a little more lenient, a little more gentle "

Naughty Dorothy squeezed out a tear or two, which, as she had fully intended, brought Arnold to his knees, figuratively. He did not actually kneel, but he gathered the little witch in his arms, and said, "Don't cry, dear. You shall have everything you want, and nothing you don't want, after we're married! There, how does that suit your little ladyship?"

"That's all right, then;" and Dorothy smiled through what was left of her two tears. "And now, Justin, you must take me back, for I've promised this dance to Mr. Chapin."

"Chapin? I say, Dorothy, it's awfully good of you to give him a dance, when you have so many more interesting men at your feet. Dance with him all you like, dear, but don't dance much with Cam Crosby, will you?"

"Jealous of your own cousin! Fie, fie! I won't promise. He has asked me for a whole heap of dances."

"I don't doubt that, but I give you fair warning: every time I see you with him, I'm coming to take you away. I only wish I could dance myself, and then no other man should have a single turn."

"You're an old fogy, Justin! You can't dance, and you can't play bridge, and you can't do much of anything gay and jolly!" Then, as a dark frown settled on her lover's face, she whispered, close to his ear, "But I love you," and then turned quickly, to find Ernest Chapin waiting for her.

"Don't let's dance; let's sit it out," he said, leading her back to the very same little veranda where she had just been with Arnold. It was a dear little nook, with moonlight gleaming through the tracery of vines, which made weird black shadows on its light stone floor.

It was secluded from passers-by, and as Chapin paused and drew Dorothy to him, in the dark of its shadows, he whispered passionately, "Dear, I can't stand it! I can't see you with him, and see his air of ownership of you!"

"But I'm going to marry him. Why shouldn't he show an air of ownership?" Dorothy spoke coldly, but she was trembling, and her large eyes lifted themselves to Chapin's face with a despairing glance.

He clasped her two little hands tightly in his own.

"You are selling yourself to him!" he exclaimed, in tense, low tones. "You know you love me, and yet you are marrying Arnold because he is rich."

"It is not so! You have no right to talk to me like that! I adore him; I worship the ground he walks on!"

"You blessed baby!" said Chapin, putting his arm around her. "The very emphasis you put on those ridiculous words proves how false they are. Dorothy, dearest, tell me just once that you do love me, and I will let you go."

"You must let me go, anyway, Ernest. Don't hold me, please don't! Justin may come back at any moment."

"I don't care. I wish he would! Dorothy, how can you marry that man, almost old enough to be your father? How can you sell yourself for wealth and high position?"

But Dorothy's senses had returned. "I'm not doing anything of the sort, Mr. Chapin, and I command you to stop talking to me like that. As you know, I never even saw you until after I was engaged to marry Mr. Arnold. If I had met you sooner—"

There was a little break in Dorothy's voice, and Chapin whispered despairingly: "Oh, darling, if you only had!"

"And now," Dorothy went on, "there is nothing more to be said on this subject, now or ever. It is not honorable in you, Mr. Chapin, nor in me. In a few weeks I shall marry Mr. Arnold, and I hope I may trust you never to say anything of this nature to me again."

"I hope you may trust me, Dorothy," said the man brokenly, "but I know I cannot trust myself."

"At least, we can try," said Dorothy, in a low voice, and then without another word they returned to the dancing-room.

"Mine!" cried Emory Gale, as he caught sight of Dorothy, and went toward her with open arms.

"What!" exclaimed Arnold, who was hovering near.

"Heavens, old man! don't kill me! I only meant this is my dance with Miss Duncan."

"Oh," said Arnold, who was miserably jealous and couldn't hide it. He dropped into a chair and watched the girl he loved enfolded in another man's arms. Not being a dancer, Arnold couldn't look on such an embrace impersonally. His reason told him that every girl on the dancing floor was necessarily encircled by her partner's arms, but that didn't take away his hatred of seeing Dorothy so close to Emory Gale. He would have objected equally to any other man, but Gale was a daredevil, and Arnold knew him better than Dorothy did. Still, he couldn't forbid her dancing with one of his own house guests, and, incidentally, one of his own lawyers. Gale and Crosby were the successors of the firm that had been his father's lawyers, and so Justin employed them, although a firm doing business in New York would often have been more convenient.

"Your little friend seems peeved," said Gale to Dorothy as they dipped and sidestepped.

"Rather!" said Dorothy, carelessly; "he can't bear to see me dance. He doesn't dance at all, you know, and he thinks it's a personal affront to him when I do. Besides, these new dances are a sort of revelation to him. When he was young, he saw the polka redowa and such things, he tells me, and then he went into his shell and never came out till he was engaged to me, and now these 'aesthetic' dances shock him all to pieces."

"But he must be educated up to them," returned Gale, as he skilfully piloted his light-footed partner among the maze of people.

"Yes," and Dorothy shook her pretty head decidedly; "for I expect to dance as long as I live."

"Let's give him a benefit lesson now, then, and help his education along as rapidly as possible!"

Gale smiled into Dorothy's eyes, and the girl understood. Both of them were excellent dancers and well versed in all the newest and most intricate steps.

Both knew how to exaggerate or prune the effects of the more conspicuous dances, and Dorothy gleefully consented to be led around toward the corner where Arnold waited for her return. She was always ready for mischief and she liked Emory Gale, but, too, she honestly wanted her future husband to realize that it was her intention to dance all she chose and as she chose, both before and after her marriage to him.

So, as they neared Arnold, their step became more daring, their pose more relaxed, and though it meant nothing to the dancers, Arnold saw it and went white with fury. Without looking at her fiance, Dorothy kept her earnest gaze on Gale, partly to watch his intended direction, and astnuch to tease the man who looked angrily after her.

"He's madder'n hops," announced Gale, cheerfully; "shall we go round again?"

Dorothy had lost her head a little in the whirling rhythm, and she only whispered, "Yes," and went on dipping and swaying to the enticing music.

"Let's do that last new 'Humoresque,'" murmured Gale, as they neared Arnold, and as they passed him, both were engrossed in the intricacies of the difficult dance.

Arnold, in his ignorance, mistook their absorption for interest in each other, and ground his teeth in rage as they went by without a look toward him.

The music stopped, and flushed and a little breathless, but indescribably lovely, Dorothy, leaning on Gale's arm, sauntered to Arnold's corner.

"There, Justy, how do you like our very latest achievement?" and Dorothy bridled with pretty vanity.

If there was one thing Arnold hated it was to be called "Justy," and Dorothy knew it. But her spirit of mischief was in the ascendant to-night, and she couldn't resist adding fuel to the flame she had already roused.

"It's absolutely disgraceful, Dorothy, and I forbid you ever to give such an exhibition again!"

"Oh, come, now, old chap," said Gale, "don't be so old-fogy and back-woodsy and hidebound "

"And old-maidish," put in Dorothy, "and dog-in-the-mangerish! Just because you can't dance, you needn't revile my skill in that direction."

"And, by Jove, skill it is!" exclaimed Crosby, who had come up. "I say, Dorothy, I never saw anyone put that through as you did! The next is ours, isn't it?"

"Indeed it isn't," laughed Dorothy, "the next is Mr. Gale's."

This was too much for Arnold. Taking Dorothy's arm a little firmly, he led her into the next room, which was the big, cosy living-room.

"Help, help!" called Dorothy, laughing over her shoulder, and Gale and Crosby followed the pair. Unafraid of Arnold when there were others present, Dorothy flung herself on a big sofa among a heap of cushions.

"Now scold," she said, looking up at her tortured lover. Who could scold such a vision of loveliness?

Her perfect arms extended along the cushions, her dainty feet crossed, and her roguish, daring face smiling with full assurance of her own power. Arnold stood in front of her, and tried to steel himself against this witchery.

"I am going to scold you, Dorothy," he began, but she interrupted, "No, you're not!" and sprang up and faced him.

There was a tense, breathless moment, as if the two wills measured against each other. Dorothy stood, one hand resting on a library table, her parted lips matching her scarlet frock, her eyes and hair black as night, and her compelling glance holding Arnold's own. Watching closely, she saw his mouth relax a trifle and she knew she had won.

The reaction left her a little embarrassed, for both Gale and Crosby were watching the scene. In her nervousness, Dorothy fingered the articles on the table, and chanced to touch a Spanish dagger lying there. It was a dangerous looking affair, and though there for the purposes of a paper-cutter, it was rarely used, and even the parlormaid touched it gingerly when dusting. Dorothy's face broke into smiles, and grasping the thing, she struck an attitude like a miniature and very modern Judith, arid cried:

"Stop looking daggers at me, Justin, or I will return your glance thus!"

With a mock-tragic gesture, she pointed the dagger at Arnold's heart, and then, tossing it back on the table, she smiled and said; "No, I'll punish you this way, instead," and rising on tip-toe she kissed him lightly on the cheek. Not yet accustomed to this volatility, Arnold looked first bewildered, then pleased, then embarrassed.

"Dorothy!" he mumbled, "before people!"

"Oh, these people don't mind; do you, boys?" and Dorothy smiled carelessly at her audience of two. Then she picked up the dagger again. "I love the feel of these things," she said, running her little forefinger lightly along the blade. "I think my ancestors were pirates and Spanish dancing girls! A stab in the dark!" and making a lunge toward Gale, she assumed the attitude of a small but very ferocious pirate.

"Dorothy! for heaven's sake, behave yourself!" cried Arnold; "put that thing down!"

"All right," and Dorothy laid the dagger in its place; "but I do feel dramatic. Mayn't I play tableaux, Justin?"

"Play whatever you like, if you don't touch that fiendish thing! I'll have it thrown away!"

"No, don't!" cried Dorothy, "I just love it! Give it to me, won't you, dear! For a wedding present? But you'll have to, if you give me 'all your worldly goods.' Well, I still feel dramatic. If I can't play with the dagger, I'll have to choose more simple themes. Mr. Gale, will you play 'Living Pictures' with me?"

"Yes, if you'll show me how, I'm at your service. What must I do?"

Gale stepped forward and stood in a waiting position.

Dorothy looked at him thoughtfully, her head on one side, like a perplexed connoisseur.

"Why," she said, laughing, "you look exactly like the man in that foolish old picture of 'The Huguenot Lovers.' See, this way."

Dorothy caught up a light couch cover and draped it over Gale's shoulder, and then, announcing, in showman-like voice, "The famous painting, 'The Huguenot Lovers,' "she threw herself into Gale's arms and assumed a most exaggerated look of despairing affection.

Gale quickly caught the allusion and cleverly took the pose shown in the well-known picture. It was over in a moment, and laughing Dorothy sprang back, saying, "I always thought I had dramatic talent; now I'm sure of it! Why don't you applaud, Justin?"

"Never mind him," said Campbell Crosby, "he's got a grouch to-night. Come, play a 'Living Picture' with me, Dorothy; what shall it be? Oh, I know! Do you remember that fearful old thing called 'Alone at Last!'?"

"Yes!" said Dorothy, laughing, "it is in my great aunt's parlor. It's like this."

Crosby, with clever caricature, reproduced the stilted pose of the hero of the old classic, and Dorothy hung around his neck in a dragging way, with a look of utter infatuation on her lovely face.

Arnold missed the burlesque effect and saw only the embrace. He rose steadily, though he felt as if the earth were rocking beneath him.

"I've had enough of this," he said, in a low, even voice, and walked slowly toward the door.

"Oh, wait, Justy," cried Dorothy, "I'm going to give 'The Conscript's Departure' next, and I want you to act it with me."

"Thank you," said Arnold, not looking at her, "I have no talent for that sort of thing. You have all the mummers you need."

"But you are acting a picture now!" called Dorothy, as he reached the door; "you're giving a splendid representation of 'The Girl I Left Behind Me'!"

Arnold strode away, and Gale said, curiously, "Aren't you afraid to stir him up like that?"

"I'd be afraid not to," and Dorothy spoke without a smile; "I must get him used to my foolishness, if I expect to have any fun at all after I'm married."

"But will you be married, if you go much further in this mad career that you're pursuing tonight?"

"Oh, yes, if I want to. I'll give Justin a little while to calm down and then I'll go and 'make up', I'm a great little old make-upper, I am."

"But he's pretty mad, just now," said Crosby, who knew Arnold thoroughly.

"No matter," and Dorothy tossed her curly head. "He's been pretty mad lots of times, but I can manage him."

"I wish you weren't going to marry him," blurted out Crosby.

"So do I,—sometimes," and Dorothy drew a sigh that might have been genuine, or merely for dramatic effect.

"If he ever scolds you I'll kill him!" Crosby declared, and Dorothy, smiling, returned, "He'll never scold me. If he does, I'll kill him, myself! Come on, there's the music again! Let's go and dance."

Chapter 5: Scolding Is Barred

"THERE'S no use talking, Justin, I have promised to be your wife, and I will; but I will not be your slave, or submit to tyranny! It is to be understood that after we are married I am to dance as much as I like and with whom I like, and you are not to scold or be grumpy about it. Do you agree?"

"But, Dorothy, these modern dances are improper."

"They are not! Everyone dances them. Do you suppose my mother would sit by and see me, if I danced improperly? And, another thing, I wish you wouldn't say, 'these modern dances,' as if you were of your grandfather's generation! Aren't you modern, yourself? I am living to-day, and so are you. You may have been born twenty years before I was, but you are now living in the same era, and you've got to act so! Won't you,—dear?" It was the morning after the dance, and it was Sunday, and the pair were strolling round the park. Dorothy, not in outing garb, but wearing a dainty little house frock of pink linen, looked very dear and sweet. She was "making up" with Arnold, and it was not a simple matter,—for she was setting the pace for her future life. She had thought it over, in her wise little head, and she knew that if she could get him to agree to certain stipulations, he would never break his word.

"I do want to be all that you want me to be, darling," Arnold said, looking troubled, "but you know,—you must know,—that there is a certain dignity expected from a married woman that is imperilled by such exhibitions as you gave last evening with Gale."

"Oh, Emory Gale! Isn't he the funniest man! I never thought a lawyer could be so frivolous! Mr. Crosby isn't."

"No, Cam Crosby is more serious. By the way, do you like him, Dorothy?"

"Who? Mr. Crosby? Yes, rather. But I like all men, Justin. Why shouldn't I? They're all so nice to me."

"Oh, child," Arnold groaned; "what can I do with you?"

"Love me," said pretty Dorothy, and held up her lovely lips for a kiss.

Rarely was she so spontaneously gracious, and Arnold caught her passionately in his arms.

"You beauty! You love! Dorothy, you do love me, don't you?"

"Of course I do, when you're good to me,—and don't scold me."

"I'll never scold you! But, dearest, you don't care for Cam, do you? He's mad about you!"

"Nonsense! He isn't. And I don't care two straws for him, if he is."

"Nor Gale?"

"Emory Gale! Why, Justin, he's in love with Leila."

"With Miss Duane? Is he?"

"Oh, neither of them have told me so, but—*I* know!" and Dorothy wagged her pretty head like a wise, rosy-cheeked owl.

"Then there's one less man for me to be jealous of," and Arnold laughed grimly.

"But what's one among a hundred?" and Dorothy smiled saucily at him. "Don't be jealous, Just, it makes an awful lot of trouble. Oh, here are the Cranes."

"Yes, here we are," said Fred Crane. "Sorry to interrupt a tete-a-tete."

"Not at all," said Mrs. Crane; "it's lucky we came, for I heard Dorothy asking Justin not to be jealous! Take my advice, Dot; let him be jealous. It keeps him in love with you."

"I don't care how jealous he is," said Dorothy,"if he won't scold me. I just simply can't bear to be scolded! And I won't stand it!" She stamped her little slippered foot, and looked at Arnold with such an adorable pout, that he had to smile at her.

But he said, staunchly, "You'll never get scolded unless you deserve it, my dear."

"Well, that's something!" put in Mabel Crane, hastily, for the clouds gathered on Dorothy's brow; "some poor wives get scolded whether they deserve it or not."

"Not you!" and fat, good-natured Fred Crane looked smilingly at his good-natured wife.

"There, Justin! See that!" cried Dorothy; "Mr. Crane wouldn't scold Mabel, no matter what she did! Promise you won't scold me, ever."

"The Arnolds never make foolish promises, Dorothy; nor do the Arnolds 'scold.' If you ever deserve reprimand, I shall certainly give it to you."

Dorothy gave up the siege, for the time. "I won't, dear," she said, in the meekest possible voice, but the smile she turned on Justin was offset by the suspicion of a wink in Mabel Crane's direction.

"We've been hunting specimens," said Fred Crane, to divert the trend of thought. He was in knickerbockers and carried a specimen case and butterfly net.

"Get anything?" asked Arnold, perfunctorily.

"Several worthwhile bits. Almost had a fine white moth, but he got away. By Jove, I should have had him, if I could have climbed your confounded wall! In heaven's name, Arnold, why the broken glass? Didn't your revered ancestors have any other place to put their old bottles?"

"Don't you make fun of Justin's revered ancestors," cried Dorothy; "they're pretty nearly my ancestors! Will they be mine, Just, when we are married? Do you endow me with them, along with your other worldly goods? Or, aren't they worldly goods?"

"Don't talk like that, Dorothy," said Arnold, gently; "please show a little reverence, for my sake, if not for your own."

"Oh, there's no pleasing my lord and master this morning! I think I'll seek fresh fields and pastures new.

Oh, look who's here! Mr. Gale! Won't you come out and play wiz me?" and dancing up to Emory Gale, she tucked her hand through his arm, and led him directly away from the others.

"I know you were in search of Leila," she said, as soon as they rounded the corner of the path through the wood. "And I'll take you to her in a minute. But I want to borrow you just now."

"I am honored and proud at this favor. What can I do for you?"

"Flirt with me. No, not now; only when Justin can see us."

"What a rogue you are!" Gale had meant to say something harsher, but he couldn't, with that dimpled face looking up into his.

"All's fair in love and war," said Dorothy, tossing her head. "I have to train Justin in my own way, you see. But never mind me; let's talk about Leila. I always try to interest my companions."

"And you think Miss Duane interests me?"

"Rath-er! And I don't wonder; Leila is a dear and a sweet."

"But do you think I interest her? That's more to the point."

"I think you do. But Leila's coy, and if you're going in to win, you ought to make a braver attack. Now, I chance to know she's at this moment on that little south balcony, and if you go right straight there, you will have an excellent opportunity to discuss the weather with her."

"And you?"

"I see Mr. Chapin approaching in the dim distance. Oh, I wouldn't dismiss you until I had a perfectly good substitute! Hoo-hool Mr. Chapin! Don't you want to take me to see the ducks?"

Ernest Chapin came forward eagerly. He said little, but his eyes shone and his face glowed as he led Dorothy toward the duck pond, while Gale went on his quest of Leila.

"Why don't you talk?" said Dorothy, a little frightened at the tense silence.

Chapin stood still, turned her around, and looked deep in her eyes. "Because I'm too happy. I've heard of a happiness too deep for words, and now I know what it means."

"Don't," said Dorothy, weakly; "don't! I can't bear it! You promised you wouldn't!"

"Oh, no, I didn't. But if I did,—if I promised it a hundred times,—I never could keep such a promise! To be with you,—alone with you! Oh, Dorothy!"

"Hush, there's Miss Abby!" and the two composed themselves just in time to smile at their hostess, who was sitting on a garden bench. "Just the one I wanted to see!" called out

Dorothy, gaily; "now you go away, Mr. Chapin, this is going to be a meeting of the Woman's Club."

Chapin bowed and went on, and Dorothy sat down beside Miss Wadsworth and patted her hand. Now Miss Abby was far from dull, and she scented trouble in the girl's manner. "Well," she said, drily, "have you quarrelled with Justin?"

"Aren't you the mind-reader!" and Dorothy looked honestly surprised. "No, we haven't exactly quarrelled, but, oh, well, Miss Abby, we're awfully different."

"Yes, you are, Dorothy, but I'm hoping your two natures will react on each other to the benefit of both."

Dorothy looked relieved. "Oh, do you think so? I'm so glad, for I've been wondering if I ought to marry him, when I'm so far from his ideal of all a woman should be."

"I wondered too, at first, but I've concluded that Justin loves you, as he never could love his 'ideal' if he had her."

"I know he loves me, but sometimes I feel so unworthy of his love. And, Miss Abby, I don't mean that *I* feel myself unworthy, but I'm so afraid he'll think I am."

The older woman smiled at this naive confession, but she said, "I understand, dear. But I think you ought to try a little harder to do and be as Justin wants you to. You love him, don't you?"

"I—I think so," faltered Dorothy, "but when he is so stern,—it makes me hate him!"

"That's a good sign," and Miss Abby smiled.

"Better hate him than be indifferent. And I really think, my dear, that your love will grow steadily and surely, the longer you live with him, and learn what a really fine, true nature he has."

So Dorothy smoothed out her temper and patted her little soul on the back, and resolved to be awfully good to old Justin and not to flirt with other men to tease him, and especially never, never to let herself be left alone with Ernest Chapin for one single little minute.

And all the rest of the day, she devoted herself to Arnold, and was so sweet and docile and altogether angelic, that her lover concluded he had at last learned the way to manage her!

Though the house-party had been asked only for the week-end, most of the guests were easily persuaded to stay a few days longer. Emory Gale and Campbell Crosby were the only ones who were unable to accept their host's invitation to remain longer at White Birches. Business called them, they declared, and they were obliged to leave at noon on Monday for Philadelphia.

Dorothy and Leila gave way to protestations of great grief at parting with them, and though the protestations were mere fooling, yet Crosby looked longingly into Dorothy's eyes, while, unconscious of this, Gale was pouring out his whole soul in a glance for Leila's benefit.

The girls had accompanied the departing guests in one of Justin's big motor-cars as far as the Fordham Heights Station. From here the men went to New York and later took the train for Philadelphia. Though usually inclined to light and desultory chatter, Gale and Crosby said little to each other during the first miles of their train ride. But after they had smoked for awhile in silence, they grew a little less taciturn and a little more inclined to be sociable.

"Hang it all!" said Gale, at last, "if I had time and opportunity, I believe I could induce that sweet young thing to be all my very own!"

"What's the matter with you?" growled Crosby. "She's going to marry Justin, and you'd better keep off!"

"Great snakes, man! I don't mean Dorothy! I mean the pretty one, the lovely Leila."

"Oh, Miss Duane. Yes, she's pretty enough in her way, but she can't hold a candle to that rosy little peach of a Dorothy."

"Dorothy is a beauty, all right, but she's too indiscriminating in her favors. She'd flirt with anybody, whether she's engaged to him or not."

"I wish she'd flirt with me," said Crosby gloomily. "But nevermind me. Are you really hit by the Duane girl? She's a thoroughbred, I admit, and I wish you luck, old man."

"But I never get a chance to see her. She lives 'way off in Ohio, or somewhere, and she's just here for the wedding festivities."

"Well, be expeditious. We'll go to White Birches again before the wedding, and she'll probably be there. I'll ask Cousin Abby to ask her, if you like. And then at the time of the wedding we'll all be at the Duncan house, I suppose, for a day or two, at least. I'm to be old Justin's best man. I told him I didn't want to, but I suppose I will. Oh, pshaw, man, if you've got any enterprise at all, you can find some way to woo and win a fair lady, without having her thrown at your head. I think she's ready to meet you half-way, anyhow."

Gale brightened up at this; but Crosby became more gloomy as he realized that Gale had a fair fighting chance, while he had none. It was about five o'clock when they reached the station in Philadelphia.

"What are you doing to-night?" asked Gale, as they parted.

"Dunno. Depends mostly on what letters and stuff I find waiting for me. We ought to get together and talk over that Herrmann case."

"Yes; where's that data I gave you to look over?"

"It's in my duffle, somewhere. I'll hunt it out when I get to the hotel."

"All right; and you'd better drop in at the club to-night. I'm going to dine there, and then I'll tell you if I've had any word from Herrmann. There's lots of detail to be attended to in that case."

"I'll call you up and let you know what I can do, later. S'long, old man."

They parted, and Crosby went directly to the hotel where he made his home. Gale had rooms in a bachelor apartment-house, but Crosby declared that a big hotel was the only place where a man could get decent service and comfortable surroundings. He nodded affably to the desk clerk, took his mail, and went directly to an elevator and up to his rooms on the third floor. He usually went up in the elevator, though, coming down, he oftener used the stairs. However, as his particular elevator-boy did not suffer financially from this state of things, no complaint was made.

Being expeditious by nature, and inherently opposed to what is known as "lost motion," he had run through his letters and was ready for his dinner at seven o'clock. As nothing in his mail offered him any more attractive occupation for the evening, he thought of going to the club to see Gale, and he telephoned him to this effect before going on to the dining-room. Then, seated alone at his usual table, he opened the evening paper and was soon lost in its contents.

A little before eight o'clock, he was called to the telephone, and answered "Hello "to Gale's greeting.

"Old chap," Gale said, "don't come over here to-night, unless you choose. I've promised to make up a rubber with some fellows, and I'm going home early."

"O. K." returned Crosby; "I was half inclined to go to the Orchestra Concert, and I believe I will. Haggensdorfer is on the programme, and I simply can't stay away. Want to drop in there, later?"

"No, I believe not. I'll play around here for awhile and slide home early. See that you get around to the office in some decent time to-morrow morning, and bring that memo."

"All right; I will. Good-by."

"Good-by;" and Gale hung up the receiver, rather relieved than otherwise at Crosby's defection, for he had made up his mind to write to Leila Duane that evening, in pursuance of Crosby's suggestion that he should hasten his wooing. And a letter like that required time and concentration of thought. However, Gale returned to his rooms fairly early, and was getting ready to turn in for the night when, soon after eleven o'clock, his telephone bell rang.

It was Crosby again, and he began his conversation with voluble praise of the concert.

"Oh, let up," said Gale. "Tell me the rest in the morning. I'm off to by-by."

"But hold on, Gale, that isn't all I wanted to say. I find I've left that memo at White Birches— had it there last night, looking over it. I had it with some other papers in an old wallet, and left the whole business on the dresser in my bedroom."

"Oh, hang it, Crosby! You do beat the dickens with your forgetfulness! How'm I ever going to make a lawyer out of you, unless you get over your carelessness?"

"Don't scold, Emory. I didn't go for to do it. And, I say, I'll telephone to Driggs right away, and he'll send it right bang over here by registered mail and special delivery and all those things."

"You'd better wait till morning to telephone— they're probably having a party or something; and I suppose we can get along without that stuff tomorrow. But you do make me mad."

"Yes, I know I do," responded Crosby cheerfully. "Guess I'll say good-night before you get any madder."

"Good-night," replied Gale shortly. "Get around to the office on time to-morrow morning."

He hung up the receiver with a jerk, for, though he was fairly good-tempered, he did get tired of his partner's continual forget fulness. But he allowed his thoughts to return to Leila Duane, and he soon forgot Crosby's deficiencies.

And when Crosby turned up Tuesday morning at nine o'clock, fully fifteen minutes ahead of time, full of apologies for his carelessness, Gale only said, "Never mind, old chap. Herrmann can wait a day or two more."

"I telephoned Driggs this morning," said Crosby, "'long about eight o'clock. He said he'd whack it right over here. Good boy, Driggs!"

"Did he—did he say—anything about—"

"About Miss Duane pining away because of your absence? No, he didn't."

"Oh, stuff!" said Gale. "Chuck it, and get to work, now that you're here."

And then the two men really devoted their thoughts and efforts to the business in hand.

CHAPTER 6: ON A BALCONY

AFTER Gale and Crosby had left White Birches, much of the life of the party seemed gone. Leila was plainly distrait. She had not failed to notice that Mr. Gale had evinced an interest in her attractive self, and she hated to have that interest cut off in its youth and beauty. As for Dorothy, she had only her fiance and his secretary to flash her smiles at, and that was a beggarly portion of men for the unlimited number of smiles she had at her disposal. And so when Leila attempted to appropriate Ernest Chapin, Dorothy showed fight.

After all, it was the old situation. Dorothy cared for Ernest Chapin, but he was poor. Justin Arnold was an old fogy, dictatorial, and a good deal of a bore, but he was rich.

Perhaps Dorothy was neither more nor less mercenary than other girls, but she had made up her mind to marry Justin Arnold, and she had no intention of allowing her heart to interfere with her plans. This, however, did not prevent her from smiling at Chapin, and Dorothy's smiles were like fuel to a flame. And so fascinating was this game, that Dorothy became more and more daring, more and more interested in Ernest Chapin, until finally her mother interfered.

"Dorothy," she said straightforwardly, "you must stop flirting with Mr. Arnold's secretary. Not only is it bad form and beneath your dignity, but you are jeopardizing your whole future. Mr. Arnold won't stand it much longer."

"How do you know, Mother?"

"I know from the way he looks at you when you're making those silly grimaces at Mr. Chapin."

"I don't think they're silly grimaces," and Dorothy cast a casually admiring glance at herself in a mirror; "and Mr. Chapin doesn't, either."

"Indeed he doesn't! He's over head and ears in love with you, if that's any satisfaction to your foolish, vain little heart! Dorothy, I wish you had more dignity."

"Now, Mother, am I a dignified type?"

What mother could help smiling fondly at this question, put by a dainty, saucy sprite, to whom the word "dignity "could not possibly be applied? But she tried to hide her admiration, and said with would-be sternness, "You must try to achieve a little, my dear, if you're going to be Justin Arnold's wife."

"' I will be good, dear mother,' I heard a sweet child say," sang Dorothy, with mischievous glances at her mother. "Honest and truly, black and bluely, I will be good—if I can!"

And then with a parting kiss and a gentle little shake of her mother's shoulders, Dorothy ran away to dress for dinner.

In a spirit of mischief, she determined to be very demure that night. She put on a simple little white frock, with knots of light green ribbon. She parted her hair, and brushing out its rebellious curls as much as possible, she drew it down over her ears, and into a loose knot at the nape of her neck, which had the effect of making her look like a very mischievous Saint Cecilia.

She checked an impulse to dance downstairs, and walked down slowly, with her hands hanging crossed in front of her, and, as she had fully expected, she met Arnold in the hall.

"Good heavens, Dorothy! what have you been doing to yourself?"

"Don't you like me?" An angelic smile was on the face upturned to his, and the corners of the dimpled mouth drooped in saintly fashion.

"Why, I don't know whether I do or not. What's it for? I never know what you're up to."

"Oh, Justin, that's the trouble! you never know anything! Why don't you have any perception or understanding, or inter—what do you call it interospection?"

"Interospection! There's no such word."

"Yes, there is; I just made it myself. It's a lovely word and it means if you love a little girl, you ought to understand what she means, even when she doesn't mean anything."

"Dorothy," and Arnold looked at her, not entirely with approbation. "I do believe there's nothing to you but frivolity!'"

Dorothy pouted. "You wouldn't say that if you loved me."

"Of course I love you, but I'm not of a demonstrative sort, so you needn't expect a foolish show of affection."

"I just love a show of foolish affection," murmured Dorothy, but Arnold went on, unheeding.

"And I'm eighteen years older than you are, so you can't expect me to imitate your childish ways."

"Oh, do imitate them, Justin, you'd look so funny! By the way, Justin, did you ever love anyone else before you loved me?"

"Don't ask foolish questions, Dorothy."

"Then give me a sensible answer."

"Very well, I will. I see no reason for not telling you that I did love somebody else, years ago; but she,—she didn't love me."

"I don't blame her much," said Dorothy, but she said it half under her breath, and Arnold, whose thoughts had flown backward, didn't hear her. And then the others joined them, and a few guests came, and the big hall became a scene of merry laughter and gay chatter. The hall was circular, and rooms rayed out from it in various directions. This plan allowed of many queer-shaped little rooms or alcoves between the larger apartments, and as, during the various improvement periods, some floors or ceilings had been raised and others lowered, the whole house was a delightful jumble of intricate and uncertain wanderings. Dorothy had discovered and appropriated for her own many of these "flirting corners "as she called them, but to-night she would have none of them. She stood demurely by Arnold's side until dinner was announced, and then walked with him straight to the dining-room, though usually they had to institute a search for her at meal times.

During dinner and indeed all the evening, she kept up her role of demure quietness, and her mother looked at her approvingly, for she thought her admonitions had been heeded.

Later in the evening, and after the dinner guests had gone, Arnold took Dorothy out for a little stroll around the grounds. The moonlight made the white birch trees even more silvery of bark, and turned their foliage to black velvet. Deep down in the ravines could be seen silver lights on the black water, and the autumn wind murmuring in the trees gave an added touch of solemn grandeur.

"It is a beautiful place," said Dorothy, a little thrilled as she stood on the South Terrace and looked down into the dark tangles of the woodland; "but not—not very cheerful, is it, Justin?"

"It is a magnificent place, Dorothy, but I fear you're incapable of appreciating it You would probably prefer Italian formal gardens and great sweeps of sunny lawn, with gay-colored flower-beds here and there."

"Well, yes," said Dorothy; "I think that would be pretty. But it wouldn't fit White Birches, would it, Justin?"

"I should say not! I'm glad you can at least realize that. Why, Dorothy, this is perhaps the finest old place in this country. That stone wall is unique, and as for that great arched gateway, I doubt if many English parks can match it. We Arnolds appreciate the grandeur and dignity of our ancestral home, and I hope and trust, Dorothy, that you, too, will learn to do so."

"Oh, Justin, you give me so much to learn! How can one little head hold it all?"

"It doesn't seem much, dear, to expect you to love and reverence this old place, that means so much to me."

"But, Just, it means such a lot to you, because you were born here and have always lived here. Now, I wasn't, and so you see, it's very different. My marrying you won't make me a born Arnold, you know."

"You're a born darling!" exclaimed Arnold, looking at her, as the moonlight came through the leaves and illumined her exquisite face.

"Do you love me, really?" and Dorothy's voice was wistful and sweet.

"More than life itself! More than I ought to, a great deal!"

These phrases didn't at all please Miss Duncan's fastidious taste in such matters. The first was hackneyed and meaningless, and the second was grudging and not nice in its implication. However, she had "an ax to grind," and she proposed to utilize the occasion.

"How dear you are," and her little fingers crept into his own. "I'm afraid I'm not good enough for you, Justin." A soft little sigh accompanied this mendacious speech.

"Dorothy, my angel! You're too good for me! I'm not sure I ought to link your beautiful young life to mine. But I will try to make you happy, dearest."

"Do you really desire my happiness?" Dorothy was in his arms now, her soft cheek against his, and her sweet voice very gentle and tender.

"Yes; you shall have anything you want,—anything!"

"I don't want much, Just. Only I do want you to promise that we needn't stay here at White Birches all the year round."

"Not stay here! Where would you stay?"

"Why, don't you think it would be nice to go to the mountains and seashore in the summer time?"

"But this is a perfect summer home, Dorothy."

"Well, just for part of the time, you know. And then, in winter, it is so bleak and drear here, I thought we could take a house in the city for the coldest months."

"Why, darling, it is glorious up here in winter! Such air, such bright crisp days, you wouldn't want to spend them in a smoky city!"

"Oh, the city isn't smoky, Justin. And then, I thought,—I hoped—you'd take me abroad every spring."

"Every spring! Dear, you're crazy! I thought, myself, we'd go abroad some time, but I'm very sure once will be enough for me!"

"Well, it won't for me; and you said I should have whatever I wanted!"

"Yes, in reason, dearest. But your talk is out of all reason!"

"And isn't your love for me out of all reason, too?" Dorothy's soft arms stole round his neck, and her lips met his.

"No!" and he unclasped her hands and put her a little away from him. "No; it is a true, strong, honest love, but it isn't unreasonable, nor does it ask of you such utter absurdities as you are asking of me. I think the moonlight has affected you. Let us go in, now; it is growing chill."

Dorothy had failed, and she was furious. But she controlled herself, determined not to show temper at Justin's attitude. She had amazed him, and she knew it, but it was the entering edge of a wedge which might be driven farther some other time. So she only said:

"Yes, let us go in. It is dignified and all that, but somehow, Justin, it frightens me. The shadows are so weird, and those ghostly white trees shiver in the wind like spectres of the departed Arnolds. Do you suppose they're wagging their branches at me because they don't like me?"

"Nonsense, Dorothy! You're enough to give a man the creeps. Come on into the house."

As the ladies took up their bedroom candles and went upstairs, leaving the men to spend a half-hour in the smoking-room, Dorothy called down from the upper landing, "Don't forget to put on the burglar-alarm, Justin. Somebody might come and carry me off."

It was characteristic of Arnold that he answered seriously, "I've never forgotten it yet, Dorothy," and ignored the latter part of her speech.

The burglar-alarm was rather a standard joke among guests at White Birches, but this had never interfered with Justin Arnold's systematic observance of the old custom.

Dorothy paused at Leila's room for a good-night gossip. She was still in a quiet mood, and Leila asked her frankly what was the matter.

"Nothing," said Dorothy, with a little sigh. "I'm going to try to give a successful imitation of the dignity of the Arnolds for the rest of my life. I must learn to behave like an Arnold if I'm going to be one."

"Perhaps," said Leila daringly, "you'd rather see than be one!"

"No, not that," said Dorothy thoughtfully.

"Justin isn't very much to see, you know."

"I think he's a very handsome man."

"Oh, handsome nothing! He has a face like a hawk, a disposition like an iceberg, and not a bit of temper. I wish he had a temper!"

"He'll probably develop one after he marries you."

"It won't be my fault if he doesn't. But he is an old duck, and I'm terribly fond of him. Now let's change the subject. How many letters have you had from Mr. Gale?"

"What do you mean?" exclaimed Leila, blushing. "He only went away this noon. He's hardly in Philadelphia yet."

"Oh, yes, he is. He reached there before six o'clock, and I've no doubt he's spent the whole evening writing letters to you and tearing them up, in a vain endeavor to strike just the right note of friendliness."

"Dorothy, you're a goose, and I wish you'd go on to bed."

"I am going, dearie, because I know you want to write to Emory Gale!"

Dodging the little white pillow that Leila threw at her, Dorothy flew out into the hall and made for her own room.

As she turned a corner of the dimly lit corridor, she felt herself suddenly grasped by a pair of strong arms and drawn quickly between some heavy draped curtains, and out on to a tiny balcony.

"'Sh!'" whispered Ernest Chapin's voice, close to her ear. "I've kidnapped you! You said some one might, so I thought I'd be the one!"

"Unhand me, villain!" whispered Dorothy, giggling at the escapade. "I decline to be drawn behind the arras and carried to who knows what fearful fate!"

"No more fearful fate than to look at the moon for two minutes. It's marvellous from this balcony, shining on that little dark pool. Come and see."

Not entirely unwilling, Dorothy let herself be led out on the little balcony, and, to do Chapin justice, the moonlight effect was quite all he had claimed for it.

Dorothy knew perfectly well she ought not to be out there alone with Ernest Chapin, but a sort of reaction had followed her demure mood, and she murmured, "Just a minute, then. I won't give you but just exactly one minute."

"Then, I shall make the most of it," said Chapin, quickly clasping her in his arms. "Dorothy, my darling, I wouldn't do this, but I know, *I* know, you love me. You don't love Arnold! And, oh, sweetheart, don't marry him! Don't sell yourself for the Arnold fortune! Come to me, dearest, for you know, you know, you love me."

The sweetness and nearness of Dorothy, and the maddening effect of the moonlight, had caused Chapin to lose all caution, and, though low, his deep tones were clear and distinct.

A cold, hard voice followed his own:

"Oh, no, she doesn't love you, Chapin. You're awfully mistaken! She may be flirting with you— it's one of her bad habits—but she doesn't love you."

"I do," declared Dorothy, irritated by Arnold's calm statements and cutting manner.

"No, you don't, Dorothy. You're a little affected by the moonlight, but you're not in love with a man who is beneath you socially, and who, incidentally, is a coward, and a traitor to the man who employs him."

"Stop!" cried Dorothy, "you shan't talk so about the man I love!"

"You hear, Arnold," said Chapin, with a laugh that was a little unsteady. He still held Dorothy in his arms, and as Arnold stepped out on the balcony, the pair faced him.

"Go to your room, Dorothy," said Arnold, quietly; "I will settle this matter with Mr. Chapin."

"I won't go, Justin, until I explain. It isn't Ernest's fault. I asked him to come out here"

Dorothy told her lie calmly, hoping to shield Chapin from the wrath she saw blazing in Arnold's eyes.

"And since when have you called my secretary by his first name? That is more than I do, myself."

"Perhaps he is more to me than he is to you!"

Dorothy's voice shook and she drew closer to Chapin, who held her to him.

"I can say nothing, Mr. Arnold," he said, and his tones were clear and strong. "I deserve your scorn and reproach; I have acted the part of a coward and a cad. My only excuse is that I love the same woman you do, and she—"

"Yes," whispered Arnold, with dry lips, "and she—"

"I'll answer for myself," said Dorothy, suddenly, "I love you, Justin!" She left Chapin's side, and nestled against Arnold. Her perfect face, uplifted in the moonlight, thrilled him, and he put his arm round her. Then as suddenly he withdrew it.

"You don't!" he cried. "You are only marrying me for my money! You are untrue, unfaithful;— a shallow-hearted coquette! You never loved me! you have deceived me with your false smiles and kisses, and as soon as my back is turned, you are caressing someone else! Our betrothal is ended. I cast you off! No Arnold has ever married a faithless woman. Go to your room. I will attend to this cur who has betrayed me!"

Ernest Chapin said slowly and clearly, "I will answer those remarks to you alone, Mr. Arnold."

"Yes; I think you will," Justin Arnold replied. "Go to your room, Dorothy. I will discuss this little matter with you to-morrow."

"Good-night, Justin," said the girl, in a small, scared voice. "Good-night, Mr. Chapin."

Neither of the men replied, and Dorothy, dazed at the situation, walked slowly to her own room.

CHAPTER 7: MISSING!

The next morning Leila Duane burst into Dorothy's room without the formality of knocking.

"What's the matter?" asked Dorothy, fixing her large, dark eyes on her friend's perturbed face.

Dorothy's own face was not smiling. She looked a little pale, and seemed weary, as if she had passed a restless and wakeful night.

Leila looked at her silently for a minute.

"Dorothy," she began, "something strange has happened—at least, we don't know whether it's strange or not."

"Well, do you know whether it's happened or not?" questioned Dorothy rather satirically.

Whereupon Leila sat down on the edge of the bed and began to cry. "Dorothy, don't be frivolous," she sobbed. "It may be something awful. They can't find Mr. Arnold."

"Can't find Justin! What do you mean? Where is he?"

"Why, we don't know! Nobody knows. Only, he's gone."

"What nonsense, to get so excited over that! Justin's old enough to take care of himself. He's probably gone to New York to buy my wedding ring."

Leila got up to go away. "Dorothy," she said, "I advise you to stop talking like that, and I advise you to get dressed and come downstairs as soon as you can."

Dorothy rang for the maid, and proceeded to make a leisurely toilet. Though not given to questioning servants, she asked the girl what she knew about Mr. Arnold's absence.

"I don't know nothing, miss. I heard Peters say that Mr. Arnold wasn't in the house or on the place, but Driggs he told us all not to say a word to anybody, and, anyhow, I don't know nothing about it, miss."

"Never mind what Driggs told you,—you tell me all you know."

"Honest, miss, I don't know nothing."

"Then why is there such an excitement because Mr. Arnold has gone away early somewhere? Has he never done such a thing before?"

"I don't know, ma'am; I've not been here very long."

"What has Driggs to do with it, anyway? It's not his business to look after Mr. Arnold's movements. Why did he tell you not to say a word to anybody?"

"I don't know, miss, but he was that particular about it!"

"Well, you don't seem to know anything! Finish hooking my frock and let me go."

But before she left the room, Dorothy made another attempt.

"Cora," she said, coaxingly, "tell me what you know. I won't tell that you told me. I'm—I'm afraid to go downstairs."

"Well, Peters said,—but I'll be discharged if I tell you, Miss Duncan. Driggs said as how we should."

"Nonsense!" and Dorothy stamped her foot."I tell you I won't let anyone know that you told me. Go on; what did Peters say?"

"He said as how Mr. Arnold has been gone all night, because his bed hasn't been slept in."

Dorothy turned white and leaned against the wall for a moment. Then she went to the mirror, scrutinized herself carefully, and turned to the maid.

"Do you think I look queer, Cora?"

"Not to say queer, miss, but sorta peaked-like."

"Peaked? I don't know what that means."

And rubbing her cheeks, and forcing a smile, Dorothy went slowly downstairs.

She found everybody assembled in the livingroom, with Miss Abby Wadsworth, as usual, conducting affairs.

Mrs. Duncan, with a very grave expression on her face, sat on a sofa, and made room for Dorothy by her side. The girl felt her mother's arm go round her, and she sat quietly, listening with the others.

"I can't understand it," Miss Abby was saying. "Peters, at what time did you go to Mr. Arnold's room this morning?"

"Shortly after nine o'clock, ma'am."

"Why did you go?"

"Well, ma'am, you see, Mr. Arnold always rings for me promptly at eight-thirty. And this morning he didn't ring, and I waited and waited until after nine, and then I made bold to go and tap at his door. I knocked three times, and he didn't answer, so I ventured to try the door. It wasn't locked, and I went in. Mr. Arnold wasn't there, and his bed hadn't been slept in. The covers were folded just as I always turn them down for him every night. His clothes were not about, and there was no sign of anybody."

"But this is very strange," pursued Miss Abby, quite as if it were Peter's fault. "Why should Mr. Arnold sit up all night?"

"I don't know, ma'am. But if he did do that same, where is he now?"

"He must be somewhere about the place," said Miss Abby decidedly. "Of course there is an explanation. He may have gone for a walk late last night, and have fallen or met with some accident."

"Excuse me, ma'am," said Driggs, "but he couldn't get out of the house."

"Why couldn't he?" inquired Mrs. Duncan.

"Because," explained Driggs, "Mr. Arnold always turns on the burglar-alarm himself every night; and I turn it off every morning. When I look at it in the morning, ma'am, the indicator would show if it had been tampered with during the night."

"Are you sure?" asked Mr. Crane, with interest.

"Yes, sir; and if a window or door had been opened during the night while that there alarm was set, there'd have been a ringin' of electric bells all over this house, a-makin' such a din as nobody could have slept through.

No, sir, that alarm wasn't touched from the time Mr. Arnold put it on last night, till I put it off this morning. And between them times, they wasn't no door nor window opened or shut in this whole house. Therefore, I says Mr. Arnold must be in the house, because he couldn't get out."

In his intense earnestness, Driggs had almost forgotten his servility of manner, and, looking straight at Mr. Crane, spoke as man to man, in the face of a great mystery. Then he turned his gaze to Miss Wadsworth, and, though she also was mystified, she nodded her head in corroboration of Drigg's statements and his conclusion therefrom.

"It is so," she said. "Justin has often explained to me how perfectly the alarm works, and how impossible it is to open an outside door or a window without starting the bells to ringing."

"Might it not be temporarily out of order?" suggested Mr. Crane, who had constituted himself Miss Abby's right-hand man and chief adviser.

"It never has been, sir," volunteered Driggs, "since I've been here, and that's nigh on to forty years. I come here a young man, when Mr. Justin was a baby; and his father was a crank, if I may say it, about burglars. He had all the wiring done and the alarm put in in his day; and, following his orders, Mr. Justin has kept the thing up, and has added a good many new contraptions as fast as they were invented. No, sir, wherever my master may be, and whatever his reason for hiding, he's in this house! 'Cause why? 'Cause he couldn't get out, without either turning off that alarm or raising a clatter; and neither of those things was done."

"Then he must be in the house," said Mr. Crane.

"This is a large and rambling structure. May he not have gone into some one of the smaller rooms, and perhaps suffered from some kind of a seizure or stroke?"

"Good gracious!" exclaimed Miss Abby. "Do you mean that Justin may be alone and unconscious, perhaps suffering, under this very roof?"

"I only mean that it might be so."

"Then let us have a thorough search made," said Miss Abby excitedly. "Peters, you know which rooms Mr. Arnold would be likely to go into—go and search them all, at once. Take some of the other servants to help you. Go all over the house, into every nook and cranny."

Peters departed, though the expression on his face showed that he hardly thought this solution of the mystery probable.

"It isn't like Mr. Arnold," began Ernest Chapin, speaking slowly, "to go into any unused room so late at night. As you know, Miss Wadsworth, Mr. Arnold is most systematic in his habits. After turning on the alarm, he invariably goes directly to his room and to bed."

"That is so," agreed Miss Abby; "but as we have to face an unusual state of things, we must admit that Justin departed from his regular systematic procedure, and we must assume an unusual occurrence of some sort."

"But it all seems so ridiculous," spoke up Dorothy; "I'm sure Justin has only gone out for a walk or a ride, and will bob in at any minute. He might have started out after Driggs took off the alarm."

"But his bed has not been slept in," Miss Abby reminded her. "Peters says he thinks Justin did not go to his room at all, as his brushes and things have not been touched since Peters arranged them for the night."

"There seems to be nothing the matter except that Justin didn't sleep in his own room," said Dorothy. "I don't think that's anything to make such a fuss about. He must have gone to New York, or somewhere, late last night, after the rest of us had all gone upstairs. Then, as he knew he couldn't get in this house during the night, he stayed in New York and he will come home on an early train."

Mabel Crane looked at Dorothy steadily. At first the girl did not see her, then when she became aware of the close observation, she flushed crimson and buried her face in her mother's shoulder.

"Who saw him last?" inquired Fred Crane, suddenly.

Dorothy lifted her head and stared at the speaker. Then she glanced round the room. Everybody was looking at Crane as if waiting for him to answer his own question.

CHAPTER 8: THE SEARCH

"WHY, I don't know," said Miss Wadsworth at last; "it must have been some of the servants, I suppose. Let me see, we ladies all went upstairs about midnight, and I suppose you men went to the smoking-room—didn't you, Mr. Crane?"

"Yes; and we stayed there, I should think, some fifteen or twenty minutes. There were only Arnold, Mr. Chapin, and myself. The night before, Gale and Crosby were here, and we had a merrier time. But last night we weren't very gay, and I went upstairs, I should say, about twelve-thirty."

"That's right," said Mr. Chapin; "we went upstairs at half-past twelve. When I left Mr. Arnold, he said he would make his tour of inspection of the house, as he always did, set the alarm, and then turn in. He must have done this, for he came upstairs not more than ten minutes after I did."

As Ernest Chapin said all this, in a slow, clear, and careful voice, he looked straight at Dorothy. The girl understood perfectly that he intended to say nothing of the scene on the little balcony, or of Mr. Arnold's appearance. She realized that he was doing this to screen her from possible unkind criticisms, for while Justin Arnold's whereabouts remained a mystery, it would be unpleasant to have a lovers' quarrel affect the question. Dorothy was grateful to Mr. Chapin for this consideration, and as of course it was assumed that all the ladies had gone straight to their rooms and stayed there, no further questions were asked about it.

But now that it was acknowledged that the disappearance was a mystery, every one began to feel a vague uneasiness that was appalling because of its very vagueness. The facts were so few and so contradictory: Justin Arnold was missing; he could not get out of the house, and yet he was not in the house. That was the case in a nutshell.

Peters returned from his search of the rooms, and announced that there was no sign of the missing man, and no sign of anything unusual or strange in any room.

"When did you see Mr. Arnold last, Peters?" inquired Mr .Crane of the valet.

"When I laid out his dinner clothes, sir; or, rather, when I attended him as he dressed for dinner."

"He seemed the same as usual?"

"Just the same, sir. I've been with Mr. Arnold for nearly ten years, and he's always been the same. A kind master, but not given to talking to his servants. As, indeed, why should he? But some masters chat a bit now and then. After Mr. Arnold went down to dinner, I put his things in order, turned down his bed, and laid out his night things, and that always ends my duties for the day. Mr. Arnold never requires me when he goes to bed. He says it only bothers him to have me about then. So my evenings are my own."

"And when do you go to Mr. Arnold's room of a morning?" Mr. Crane had taken upon himself the right to institute this investigation, and asked his questions with the air of one in charge of a case.

"I never go, sir, until Mr. Arnold rings," Peters answered; "but he always rings for me at half-past eight. This morning he didn't; and as it was the first time such a thing had ever happened, I was surprised. I waited and waited, and then, something after nine o'clock, I went to his room, and found he hadn't been there all night."

"He may have been there," objected Mr. Crane.

"Well, sir, if he was, he left no trace. Not a brush was touched, or anything on his dresser, or in his bedroom or bath-room. Of course he may have been in the room and gone away again, but he didn't sleep there last night. And "—Peters paused impressively—"he isn't in this house now, sir. I'll swear to that. I took two of the footmen, sir, and we've scoured the whole house, and there's no sign of Mr. Arnold anywhere."

"Of course there isn't!" exclaimed Dorothy.

"He wouldn't go and hide in some cupboard, and, if he had a stroke of apoplexy or anything, he couldn't have disappeared after it. I tell you he went out for some perfectly sensible reason, and he'll come back when he gets ready. I don't care anything about your burglar-alarm! If it's so clever and ingenious, he probably had some equally clever way to turn it off and on as he chose."

"But, Miss Duncan," said Driggs respectfully, "besides the burglar alarm, every door and window is fastened on the inside. The doors have heavy bolts and chains, and the windows have patent fastenings. These were all intact this morning, when I came downstairs."

"All but one, Driggs," said Dorothy, smiling.

"The one Mr. Arnold went out at couldn't have been fastened this morning, although you think it was."

Driggs said nothing, but looked unconvinced, and Mr. Crane suggested, "He has so many clever mechanical contrivances, perhaps he could open a door or window and then fasten it behind him."

"But there'd be no sense to it," said Ernest Chapin impatiently. "Why should a man like Mr. Arnold leave his house secretly in the dead of night? As his secretary, I am conversant with his business affairs, and there is nothing among those that could call him away on a secret errand. And if he had a secret errand, he was at liberty to go and attend to it, unquestioned, in broad daylight."

"What, then, do you think is the solution of this mystery?" asked Mr. Crane.

"I don't know," replied Chapin. "It seems to me that he must be in the house, although, of course, Peters has made a thorough search."

"He can't be in the house," declared Miss Abby.

"I don't care anything about thorough searching; if Justin were in the house, he'd be in someone of the rooms where he reasonably belongs. He went out of the house, that's what he did!"

Every time this opinion was expressed, Driggs seemed to consider it an imputation against his own fidelity and veracity. His long period of service had given him certain privileges above those of an ordinary butler, and he allowed himself to volunteer a remark.

"Miss Wadsworth," he began, "may I say that if Mr. Arnold did get out of this house, which he couldn't do unbeknownst, the watchman must have seen him do so? Would you, ma'am, call Malony and ask him?"

Glad of the new suggestion, Miss Wadsworth ordered that Malony be summoned at once. The big Irishman appeared, and, at a nod from Miss Abby, Mr. Crane questioned him.

"You are the night watchman on the estate?"

"Yis, sor; I'm Malony, the night watchman.

I've pathrolled these grounds ivery night for manny years."

"Do you walk all round the place, systematically?"

"I do thot! It's me dooty to poonch the timeclocks ivery half-hour."

"And where are the time-clocks?"

"Well, sor, there's wan at the gatekeeper's lodge, wan at the shtables, wan each at the four sides of the house and the four corners of the grounds; betune 'em all, I'm all over the grounds all the time, and nobody, least of all the masther, would be sthrollin' around without me knowin' of it."

"But if he had left the house, Malony, when you were in a distant corner of the grounds, you might not have seen him."

"Thrue for ye, sor; but thin, be the same token, I'd run across him sooner or later, in me thrips, fer he couldn't get out of the grounds. The big gate is locked and barred so strong that it wud take a batterin'-ram to break it down. And this marnin' ivery one of thim bolts and bars was jist as they should be. So I puts it to ye, sor: cud anny man get out of that gate and bolt and bar it behind him? He cud not! And cud he get over the wall? ye'll say. He cud not! The wall is tin feet high, and the top av it is dekkyrated wid' the foinest collection of broken bottles to be found in the country. Their p'ints stick up as jagged and sharp as so many swoord-blades, and if anny man cud manage to climb over that wall, he'd be in ribbins when he kem down on the other side! Would Mr. Arnold do thot? He wud not! And so it's plain, sor, that Mr. Arnold did not come out av his house, which he couldn't get out av; and did not purrood about his grounds, because, forbye, he isn't there!"

Malony's voice, at the last, dropped to a mysterious and meaningful whisper, so that Crane was moved to inquire, "What do you mean by saying so emphatically that Mr. Arnold is nowhere on the grounds?"

"Becuz I searched ivery where! Me and two of the gardeners and some of the stable-b'ys, we've been scouring the grounds iver since we heard Mr. Arnold was missin', and, though we've looked in ivery ravine and holler, he jist ain't there!"

Mr. Crane rather prided himself on his "detective instinct," and he caught at what he considered a point.

"If Mr. Arnold couldn't get out of the house, Malony, why did you go to the trouble of making such a thorough search of the grounds?"

Malony's honest fact looked grave. "Perhaps it was raysonless, sor," he said, "but them grounds is my special charge at night And though Mr. Arnold cuddent get out of the house without Driggs knowin' it, yet I thought it was up to me to make sure that he wasn't in the grounds, in case I shud be asked the question."

To more than one mind present, this was a slight indication of a possible complicity on the part of Driggs. The only evidence that the burglar-alarm had not been switched off and on again while Arnold went out, was Driggs's word to that effect. But closely allied to that came the thought that if Driggs were not telling the truth, Malony might be equally mendacious!

However, there was no real reason to suspect these old servants. For years they had been trusty and true, and any hypothesis leading toward an idea that they connived at or assisted Justin Arnold's secret departure from his own home was too melodramatic and absurd to be considered for a moment.

The servants were dismissed, and the little group in the library looked at one another blankly, while considering what to do next.

"Of course, only two things are possible," declared Fred Crane, emphasizing his statement by pounding his right fist into his left palm.

"What are they?"said his wife, as he seemed to be awaiting the question.

"One is," and again came the emphatic pound, "that Arnold is on some perfectly plausible and natural errand somewhere—"

"Which of course he is!" interrupted Dorothy, her eyes blazing as she spoke.

"Or else," went on Crane, "those two men servants know where he is."

"Which two?" said Chapin.

"Driggs and Malony. Yes, and I will include Peters. If any harm has come to Arnold, those men are responsible. For it is clear on the face of it, Arnold couldn't leave the house or grounds without their knowledge. And he has left,—that is also clear. Now the only question is, why did he leave and where is he?"

"And I hold that it is none of our business," said Chapin. "If Mr. Arnold chooses to go away without announcing his intention, he has surely a right to do so. And if for any reason he wanted to preserve secrecy, and for that end took his servants into his confidence that, too, is not our affair. For my part, I refuse to consider the matter a mystery, unless he remains away an unreasonable length of time."

"I think you're wrong, Mr. Chapin," said Mabel Crane. "I'm sure Peters was absolutely honest in his surprise at not finding his master" in his room, and I am equally sure that the other two men are not playing a part."

"Yet what other conclusion can we come to?" said Chapin, a little testily. "Have you anything else to offer? Personally I am not at all sure that the servants connived at Mr. Arnold's departure. But it doesn't matter. Mr. Arnold is not here, it is for us to await his return, but not to speculate as to his whereabouts."

"I agree with you, Mabel," said Leila Duane, who had kept silence while the others had discussed the matter. "I think anyone could see at a glance that those servants spoke the truth. If Mr. Arnold had gone away secretly and told them not to tell, it would have been because of some joke or little surprise for us, and the servants would have been mysterious or enigmatical, but indifferent. Those men were scared,—that's what they were,—scared. Now I tell you something has happened to Mr. Arnold, and we ought to investigate at once. And even if I am wrong, no harm can come of it."

Fred Crane looked at her. "Sensibly spoken, Leila!" he said; "but how shall we go about an investigation? What can we do, more than has been done?",

"Nothing has been done. To ask two or three servants to look over the place is not investigating. Someone must take the lead, but surely I am not the one to do it."

As head of the house, in Arnold's absence, Miss Wadsworth was looked to for directions or suggestions. But the poor lady had no suggestions to offer.

Ernest Chapin, as confidential secretary of the missing man, seemed next in authority, but, like Miss Abby, he was agitated and unnerved at the situation. Most of the time he sat with head bowed, as if deeply depressed, and when spoken to he looked up with a start, and his face expressed a horror of uncertainty that seemed to add a deeper tone to the tragedy—if tragedy there were.

Dorothy Duncan persisted in treating the matter lightly. "I know Justin better than any of you," she said; "and I know just what he would do and what he would not do. And I know that he would not do any of the absurd things that you people seem to think he has done. He would not sneak out of his house at night, either with or without the assistance of his servants, knowing that it would throw all of us into this state of wonder and dismay. He would be too considerate of Miss Wadsworth and of—of myself, to do such a thing!"

CHAPTER 9: NOT FOUND

"THEN, where is he?" spoke up Fred Crane crisply.

"I don't know where he is; but I know he is on some perfectly plausible and commonplace errand. He has probably been delayed, but he will return shortly, and as soon as he possibly can."

Fred Crane was a little disconcerted at this rational way of looking at the matter, for already he had pictured himself doing clever detective work in what gave promise of being a mystery, if not a tragedy.

Somewhat reassured by Dorothy's practical remarks, Miss Wadsworth began to reason. "I really agree with you, Dorothy," she said, "or, rather, I should do so if I did not know far better than you do, my child, about the positive efficiency of the burglar-alarm. Why, once I went downstairs, one hot summer night, and unfastened and opened a library window. Scores of electric bells whirred all over the house, and the servants seemed fairly to spring up out of the floor, they collected so rapidly I—I think with you that Justin did get out somehow, but not unless that alarm had been turned off."

Fred Crane put on his thinking-cap at this. Could it be that Miss Wadsworth suspected Driggs's veracity. But he hardly dared even hint at this, so he rather cleverly made another suggestion.

"As so much seems to hinge on the evidence of that burglar-alarm," he said, "why not send for an electrical expert of the right sort, and let him examine it?"

"That is a fine idea!" exclaimed Miss Abby, who really had been forced to let a suspicion of Driggs creep into her mind, though she fought against it.

"And if I may make a suggestion," said Mrs. Duncan, in her quiet way, "I propose that we send for Mr. Arnold's physician. I can't help thinking that Justin may have had a stroke of some sort, and be unconscious and helpless even now. His doctor could tell us if he were subject to anything of the sort."

"I know he isn't subject to anything of the sort," said Miss Abby thoughtfully, "but I think yours is a good idea, Mrs. Duncan. We will send for Doctor Gaspard, and at least he can tell us if he ever feared anything like that for Justin. Let us also send for an electrical expert, or whoever it is that examines complicated machinery. Who would such a man be? Do you know, Mr. Chapin?"

Ernest Chapin looked up with a start. "Why, yes—yes," he said, as if striving confusedly to bring his mind to bear on the question. "I—I think, Miss Wadsworth, we might send direct to the firm who put the alarm in, and ask them to send us a capable man for the purpose."

"Yes, do so," cried Fred Crane. "Let us telephone for him. We must make search for Arnold, and we cannot do so intelligently until we understand more about the working of that alarm. I'm sorry, but I cannot believe, with Miss Duncan, that Arnold has gone off casually, and will soon return. I think the mystery is deeper than that, and I think, too, it is exceedingly wise to call in the family physician. There are other things than strokes or seizures that work harm to a man."

Then Mabel Crane spoke out, voicing the thought that had been secretly in the mind of every one.

"Oh, Fred," she cried, almost hysterically, "you don't mean suicide!"

"Hush, hush, Mabel," admonished her husband. "We've no reason to think of such a thing. Justin was happy, and on the eve of his marriage to the girl he loved. Why should he dream of self-destruction just now, of all times?" It had been in Mr. Crane's mind, but when his wife put it into words, the idea seemed so impossible that he repudiated it at once. But, by a sudden mutual impulse, Dorothy and Ernest Chapin looked at each other for the briefest moment, and then looked away again.

Mabel Crane intercepted the glance and they both saw her.

Dorothy flushed scarlet, but Chapin turned white. Then, apparently with an effort, he drew himself together, and taking some letters from his pocket he began to look them over.

Miss Wadsworth responded to Mabel's suggestion.

"No," she said, very decidedly, "the Arnolds do not commit suicide. Of course there is no reason why Justin should do so, but if there were a thousand reasons for it, he would not do it. I know him well, and a stronger, braver, truer man does not live.

You know this, Dorothy?"

"Y—yes," stammered the girl. "Yes, Miss Abby, of course I know—know it. Justin is a splendid man,—a fine man, "and then bursting into tears, she again hid her face in her mother's arms.

"I don't see, Dorothy," said Mabel Crane, "if you are so positive nothing has happened to Justin, why you are so overcome."

"And I don't see why it should interest you!" and Dorothy, sitting upright, looked at Mrs. Crane almost angrily. "Of course, I know Justin is all right, but you all drive me crazy with your talk about suicide, and 'something happening'! I don't wonder I'm upset! You would be, too, if people were looking at you and then looking at each other, and then nodding their heads as if—as if—"

"As if what?" demanded Mrs. Crane, with spirit.

But Dorothy's anger faded. "Nothing, Mabel. Don't mind me. I don't know what I'm saying:"

"Then you'd better not say anything," and Mabel Crane looked sternly at her.

At this juncture, Driggs returned to the library, and, going to Miss Wadsworth, showed her a somewhat worn brown leather pocketbook.

"It's Mr. Crosby's, ma'am," said Driggs. "He left it in his bedroom, ma'am, when he went away yesterday. And he telephoned me this morning, ma'am, from Philadelphia, as how it contained valuable papers, and would I ask Mr. Arnold to send it to him at once, by registered mail. That would be about eight o'clock, ma'am, that he telephoned, and I told him I would tell Mr. Arnold. And then, ma'am, in the excitement, I forgot all about the matter until just now. Will you send it to him, ma'am, or will Mr. Chapin?"

"Certainly," replied Miss Abby, taking the pocketbook and handing it to Ernest Chapin.

"Please attend to it, Mr. Chapin, and get it off as soon as possible. The delay may trouble Mr. Crosby."

"Certainly," said Ernest Chapin, taking the wallet. But he sat fumbling with it absentmindedly, as if his thoughts were far away.

"There's another thing," said Leila Duane: "as Mr. Crosby and Mr. Gale are Mr. Arnold's lawyers, perhaps they may know something about him. Perhaps he went to Philadelphia to see them."

"He didn't go to Philadelphia," said Fred Crane, a little weary of the reiteration, "because he couldn't get out to go anywhere; but I think Gale and Crosby ought to be notified about what has happened."

"There hasn't anything happened," insisted Dorothy. "At least, nothing that ought not to happen. But I do believe that Justin did go to New York to see a lawyer. Don't tell me he couldn't get out! He must have gotten out! And there's just where he's gone! He told me he wanted a will made, and he didn't want Mr. Crosby or Mr. Gale to draw it up."

"Why not?" asked Fred Crane, in astonishment. "They're his lawyers."

"Yes, I know; but you see, he wanted to leave Mr. Crosby quite a sum of money, and he didn't want to leave Mr. Gale anything; you know Mr. Crosby is related to him and Mr. Gale isn't. Well, anyway, he said it would be less personally embarrassing to go to some other lawyer. He spoke of someone in New York; I forget the name."

"I never heard of such nonsense!" declared Crane. "Gale couldn't expect anything, and of course Crosby would."

"Justin was always sensitive about such matters," said Miss Abby; "it's just like him."

"Well, whether it's like him or not," said Dorothy, "it's what he told me he was going to do. I suppose he has a right to do as he chooses in such matters!"

"Of course, child," said Crane; "don't flare up over it! No one is blaming you. But granting all that, why would a man go off in the middle of the night to get a will made? It's preposterous!"

"But what isn't preposterous as a solution of his disappearance?" said Leila.

"I'm sure that's what he did do," persisted Dorothy. "He took a notion to go to New York, and he went."

"Well, I advise notifying Mr. Gale and Mr. Crosby of the situation," said Crane. "I for one don't feel satisfied to sit and do nothing. I may be mistaken, but I think we ought to stir around a little.And perhaps Arnold has gone to Philadelphia to see his lawyers there."

"That's too ridiculous," said Dorothy; "why would he do that, when they were just here yesterday?"

But she flushed as she spoke and her lip trembled. Then she tossed her head defiantly, and said, "Do whatever you like. I'm sure I've no objections to any investigation,—as you call it."

"Doing anything is better than doing nothing," declared Miss Abby. "Mr. Crane and Mr. Chapin, I wish you would do all the telephoning, please. Get the electrical man and the doctor, and then get a long distance to Philadelphia and see if Mr. Gale knows anything about Justin."

"Better get Gale first," said Mr. Crane. "If Arnold is there, there's no use of getting in experts of any sort."

"That's so," agreed Ernest Chapin, and the two men went away to telephone.

"I shall hunt for a note," said Dorothy, jumping up; "come on, Leila, let's see if we can't find one, and get ahead of all these smart people."

But their search was unsuccessful. Though they looked in probable and improbable places, no missive was found explaining the mysterious absence of the man of the house. Imbued with the spirit of search the girls wandered through the old mansion, peering into many unused rooms, poking into dark closets and cupboards, and even going up into some of the dusty old attics.

"Perhaps, like that Ginevra Lady, he hid in an old oak chest, and the cover snapped shut, and he couldn't get out," suggested Leila, as she lifted the lid of a dusty old chest that looked as if it had been undisturbed for years; "don't you remember, Dorothy, how the girl did that on her wedding eve, and they never found her for years afterward?"

"Oh, Leila, don't say such dreadful things!" exclaimed Dorothy, shuddering.

"Why, you needn't care; you think he's just gone out for a walk, or something. *I* think something dreadful has happened to him.".

"What thing dreadful could happen to him?" and Dorothy sank limply down on a dusty old hair trunk, for the forlorn and lonely dark attic with its blackened beams and dark cobwebby corners got on her nerves. "Come on, Leila, let's go downstairs, for pity's sake!" and Dorothy made a rush for the staircase, catching Leila's hand and dragging her along with her.

"What's the matter, Dorothy? Did you see a ghost?"

But this ill-timed suggestion only added to Dorothy's terror, and she flew downstairs to the bright, beautiful library, and nestled close to her mother's side on the sofa where Mrs. Duncan was still sitting.

"Have you heard from Mr. Crosby?" Dorothy asked, breathlessly.

"Or Mr. Gale?" supplemented Leila, and then, fearful lest she might be thought to show too much personal interest, she added, "he's the senior member of the firm, isn't he?"

This ruse deceived nobody, for all present knew that Leila and Mr. Gale were more than interested in each other.

Mr. Crane answered both girls by saying, "Yes, we reached them by telephone. I talked with Mr. Gale, and he said they had seen or heard nothing of Arnold. He thinks the situation most extraordinary, and he says they will both come here at once, as he thinks such a course advisable."

"I'm glad of it," said Dorothy, "if they can help us in anyway. But I don't think we shall ever see Justin again."

"How silly you are, dearie," said her mother; "of course we shall see him again, and I hope soon."

"When will Mr. Gale and Mr. Crosby arrive?" asked Leila, for she was already considering in what gown she would better array herself.

"Gale said they'd leave on the three o'clock express. They can't get here much before seven—just in good time for dinner," said Mr. Crane, who had now definitely assumed the dictatorship. He was partly pushed into this position by Ernest Chapin's inability to pull himself together enough to be of any use. Indeed, the young secretary almost acted as if tragedy had already befallen, instead of merely an unspoken dread of it. He looked about with a vacant stare; when spoken to, he started suddenly, and then replied at random. His eyes looked frightened and vacant at the same time. He begged Mr. Crane to do the required telephoning, for he said he really didn't feel up to it.

"Don't take it so hard, Chapin," Fred Crane had responded, "I don't think anything untoward has happened to old Justin; but if that should be the case, it can't affect you as deeply as it would Dorothy and Miss Wadsworth. So brace up and do what you can to help."

Chapter 10: Dorothy's Promise

BUT though the men from Philadelphia could not reach White Birches until seven o'clock, the doctor and the electrical engineer arrived during the afternoon hours.

Their information proved of no help in solving the mystery, but rather deepened it.

After a thorough and careful examination of the burglar-alarm and all its attachments, annunciators and indicators, the electrical expert pronounced it the most marvellous affair of its kind he had ever seen.

He said that it was in perfect order, and that, owing to its wonderful and ingenious mechanism, it was positively impossible that anyone should have gone out of the house between 12.30 A.M., when it was turned on, and 7.30 A.M., when Driggs had turned it off. The man staked his entire reputation as an electrical expert on the positiveness of this statement; after which there was of course nothing to do but to theorize that Justin Arnold was still under his own roof, although this seemed equally impossible.

As to Doctor Gaspard, he simply pooh-poohed any suggestion that there was any flaw in Arnold's physical constitution or mental equipment. While, he said, a stroke of apoplexy or paralysis might happen to anyone, yet some were far more liable to it than others, and Justin Arnold was the farthest possible removed from the type of constitution that would indicate that sort of thing. He, too, was willing to stake his professional reputation that whatever had happened to Arnold, if anything, was not a physical seizure of any kind. Nor was it any variety of mental derangement. Justin Arnold's brain was not of a sort to give way in an emergency, or under mental pressure of any kind; and, moreover, no emergency or mental pressure had transpired that would even hint at such a condition.

"He is one of the soundest-minded men I know," concluded Doctor Gaspard, "and while I agree with you all that it is most mysterious, yet I must suspect the fallibility of a perfect machine before I can admit a hypothesis implying sudden dementia on the part of Justin Arnold."

"And that's where it stands," said Fred Crane, thoughtfully; "either Arnold's strong, well-balanced brain gave way, or else his infallible burglar device did. Both these things are pronounced impossible by experts,—so what is there left to think?"

As the electrical expert was still present, he looked upon this speech as a direct implication that he had misunderstood or misrepresented the infallibility of the burglar-alarm. Being of a somewhat choleric nature, he chose to take offence at this and remarked heatedly that for his part he would sooner suspect the strongest mind in the strongest body in the world, than the fallibility of a perfect machine!

"And a perfect machine it is," he went on, earnestly. "You ladies and gentlemen who are unacquainted with the real working of such a marvellous piece of ingenuity, cannot expect to understand how wonderful and beautiful its various perfections are. But you may take my word for it, as an experienced electrician, there never has been anything finer made of its kind; and you may be convinced that it is a physical impossibility for Mr. Arnold to have left this house secretly while that alarm was on."

The old doctor sniffed, and the young electrician glared back at him. Mr. Crane strove to reconcile the irreconcilable, by saying: "Then we must conclude that since Arnold was sane and in his right mind, and since he could not get out of this house, that he must still be in the house, and that of his own knowledge and volition he is hiding himself from us. We have searched the house thoroughly; but I suppose there is a possibility of some secret passage or hiding place where he might be hidden, though I can conceive of no reason for such an act."

Old Doctor Gaspard rose stiffly. "I cannot acquaint you with Mr. Arnold's reasons for what seems to be an eccentric performance, but I can assure you that whatever Mr. Arnold is doing, he knows perfectly well why he is doing it. As I assume I cannot help you further in what must necessarily now become a search for the missing man, I will ask you to excuse me."

With a disdainful glance at the electrician, whom he considered his rival in the mere question of expert evidence, Doctor Gaspard made his adieux and went away.

The electrician, concluding that his usefulness was also at an end, followed, and the members of the household were again left to confront the ever deepening mystery of the disappearance of Justin Arnold.

Though appalled by the situation, Fred Crane was taking a lively interest in this opportunity to test his detective powers, and though he had as yet accomplished nothing positively, yet he had the negative evidence of the two experts who had been called in, to work upon.

"It's just this way," he said. "Arnold must be somewhere. He couldn't get out of the house, so he must be in the house. We've not been able to find him, so we are forced to the conclusion that there is some kind of a secret passage by which he has access to the outer world. This is not an unprecedented case. In many old houses like this there are secret and subterranean passages unsuspected by chance observers."

"But not in this country," remarked Mrs. Duncan. "I've never heard of such things over here."

"But there is no other explanation, Mrs. Duncan," went on Crane, earnestly; "the process of elimination leaves that the only possible explanation of Justin's disappearance. He couldn't go up a chimney; he didn't go out of any door or window, and since he is not in the house, he must have left by some secret passage. Do you not agree with me?"

"I suppose so," said Mrs. Duncan, agreeing only because she had no other possibility to suggest.

"Well, if that's true," put in Mabel, "I'll find that secret passage! If there's one in this house, I'll find it. If there's anything in this secret passage idea, then it must be that Justin went through his secret door and the lock sprung, or something, and he couldn't get back. But he isn't hiding on purpose; and if he's walled up anywhere, I'll get him out if I have to pull the walls down!"

"Don't go to pulling the walls down, Mabel," said her husband; "when Mr. Crosby comes, he can tell us if there's any secret passage. I've often heard him say that he knows every nook and cranny of the whole place."

"Yes, he does," said Miss Abby; "as a child he was always rummaging around in the attics and cellars, and if there's any subterranean passage he'll know of it."

"Then there's nothing to do but to wait until Mr. Crosby comes," said Ernest Chapin, thoughtfully.

"But it seems awful to do nothing," said Fred Crane. "Suppose we telephone for a detective."

"Oh, mercy, no!" exclaimed Miss Abby, "I have a perfect horror of detectives! Do let us wait until Mr. Crosby and Mr. Gale come; I'm sure they can do something."

"I'm sure I don't know what they can do more than we can," declared Mr. Crane, who felt his own services unappreciated; "come, Mabel, let us go for a walk through the grounds,—we may find something by way of a clue."

The party dispersed, only to congregate again in small groups here and there, to discuss the mystery. Ernest Chapin asked Dorothy to go out on the South Terrace with him for a little chat, and, after a moment's hesitation, the girl complied. They found themselves alone on the terrace, and Dorothy said, "You don't think, do you, Mr. Chapin, that Justin's absence has anything to do with last night's scene?"

"What scene do you mean?" said Chapin, looking exceedingly perturbed.

"Why, the scene he made when he found you and me out on the little balcony, looking at the moon."

"*I* wasn't looking at the moon," said Chapin, and he turned away his eyes as he added in a low voice, "I was looking at you."

"Never mind what you were looking at," said Dorothy, blushing a little. "He spied us while you were looking; and I'm asking you if you think that circumstance had anything to do with his disappearance."

"How could it?" demanded Chapin savagely. "Do you suppose he went off and hanged himself because he saw me kiss you?" And then he added bitterly, "I only wish he had!"

"Oh, Mr. Chapin, how can you talk like that?" And Dorothy turned her lovely, frightened face toward him.

"Forgive me, Dorothy; I oughtn't to have spoken like that. I don't know what I'm saying. This thing has unnerved me."

"Then, you too think something awful has happened to Justin?"

"I don't see how anything could happen to him, but I can't believe in a casual explanation of his absence. Can you?"

"No—if he were away on some errand, he would send word to me, somehow. He wouldn't leave me in suspense all this time."

"Unless he is angry with you," suggested Chapin.

"Well, if he is, Mr. Chapin, it's all your fault!" and Dorothy's eyes blazed with indignation.

"Then I'm glad of it," said Chapin exultantly.

"If he's angry at you because he saw us together last night, and has gone away for that reason, I'm glad of it; and the longer he stays away, the better I'll like it!"

This speech did not seem to rouse Dorothy's ire as it should have done. Looking at Chapin gravely, she said, "What did Justin say to you last night after I left you?"

For a long time Chapin did not reply, and then when the silence had become almost unbearable he answered, "Nothing of any importance. And, Dorothy, be advised by me in this matter: never mention to any living soul that you and I were on the balcony last night, or that Arnold discovered us there. Will you promise me this?"

"Why?" and Dorothy's face looked troubled: "it may have been imprudent, but it wasn't a—a crime."

Chapin regarded her gravely. "Dorothy, dearest, I am very much in earnest. You must not,— you shall not tell anyone of that episode. I forbid it!"

"I am not accustomed to being forbidden!"

"Then I beg it; I implore that you will give me your promise. Do, Dorothy, do!"

The man's intensity of appeal startled her.

"Why?" she asked again.

"Never mind why. This mystery of Mr. Arnold's disappearance is not to be cleared up in a moment. And in his absence I am going to take care of you."

"What do you mean?" and Dorothy's eyes were big and frightened.

"Don't ask me what I mean! Just promise what I ask!"

"Yes,—I promise; "she spoke in a whisper as if hypnotized by Chapin's dominant personality.

"Indeed, I have no wish to tell anyone of that scene. I went to,—I mean,—I meant to tell Justin this morning that such a thing should never happen again."

"But it shall happen again!" said Chapin, and, though he spoke in low tones, his voice had an exultant ring in it that startled Dorothy.

"What do you mean by that?" she breathed.

"I mean what I say! I told you last night you should never marry Arnold, and you shan't! You are mine, mine, and, whether Arnold returns or not, you shall never marry him, but you shall marry me! Because, Dorothy, because—you love me!"

Disregarding the real tenor of his speech, Dorothy caught at a phrase.

"Whether Justin returns or not," she repeated.

"Why do you say that? Then, you do think something has happened to him!"

"I can't say," said Chapin, speaking more gently.

"It's a mystery, dear, a deep mystery. But I doubt if it is solved very soon."

And then Mrs. Duncan appeared, and carried Dorothy off to her room to rest.

"What do you think, Mother?" asked the girl, when they were alone.

"I don't know, darling. There seems no explanation whatever; but of course there must be one soon. Meantime, my child, I want you to be more careful in your behavior. You must not flirt with that Mr. Chapin. I know you don't mean anything—flirtation is second nature to you—but, my dear child, it won't do! In Justin's absence I shall look after you as carefully as he would if he were here, and I cannot allow you to play at love-making with Mr. Chapin."

"It isn't playing, Mother," said Dorothy, in a low voice.

"What do you mean by that, Dorothy?"

"I mean that it isn't playing, because it's real. I do love him, Mother, and I don't love Justin."

"Why, Dorothy, you do!"

"No, Mother, I don't. When I engaged myself to him, I thought I loved him; or, at least, I liked him as well as anybody. But I hadn't met Mr. Chapin then; and now—"

"Now you think you love him better than Justin! Dorothy, I'm not going to scold you, because you don't know your own mind, and you really imagine this state of things. But I'm going to forbid you ever to be alone with Mr. Chapin, and I'm going to command you to stamp out whatever affection you may think you feel for him. As Justin's promised wife, your faith and loyalty are due to him, and I know you must see for yourself that it is unfaithful and disloyal to treat Mr. Chapin as anything more than a mere acquaintance and your future husband's secretary."

Dorothy nestled in her mother's embrace, feeling, as she always did, the loving security of it.

"But suppose, Mother, that Justin never comes back."

"Dorothy! What an idea! Of course he'll come back! Why shouldn't he?"

"Well, but you know it's pretty queer. He couldn't have been kidnapped, and wherever he is, he ought to telephone me—or—or something." Dorothy flung herself on her bed, and burst into violent sobs.

"Now, Dorothy, sit up and be sensible. When we learn that something has happened to Justin it is time enough for you to cry like that. Stop it, now, and look forward to. his return. Let me bathe your forehead with violet water."

"I don't want any violet water! Go 'way, Mother! I want to be alone,"

"Well, you can't be. I won't leave you like this. You're unstrung, dearie, but a little nap will set you right."

Mrs. Duncan soothed Dorothy, stroking her brow gently, until the girl did fall asleep. But she woke with a start, crying: "Oh, what will Mother say when she knows!"

Mrs. Duncan was startled, but said, calmly, "There, there, dear, what were you dreaming about?"

Dorothy sat up, her eyes wide and staring, her cheeks white.

"What did I say, Mother,—what did I say?" she asked, a little wildly.

"Nothing of importance," said her mother, smiling at her. "Now, dear, you must conquer this nervousness, and get dressed. A refreshing bath and a pretty frock will make you all over. What shall you wear? Pick out a frock Justin likes, for I've no doubt he'll be home to dinner."

"Why, Mother, you speak as if he had only run down to New York on an errand."

"And very likely that is just what he has done. Now mind, Dorothy, no more flirtation with Mr. Chapin."

"I'll promise you that I'll never flirt with Ernest Chapin again; but until Justin does come back, I must have somebody to talk to."

"You're a little rogue," said her mother, kissing her fondly, "and as I'm here to look after you, I'm not much afraid that you'll do anything very dreadful. But I forbid you ever to be alone with Mr. Chapin for a moment, and I shall see to it myself that my commands are obeyed. Now you must get dressed for dinner, dearie. What shall you wear?"

"I don't know," returned Dorothy thoughtfully. "I don't feel like wearing bright colors, for it seems, somehow, as if Justin were dead."

"Don't talk like that," said Mrs. Duncan peremptorily. "Put on your rose and silver. If we feel down-hearted, that's all the more reason we should look as cheerful as possible. And probably Justin will come home to dinner, anyway, and he likes you in that dress."

"He likes me in anything; but he doesn't love me in anything. At least, not what *I* call love."

As these words were half-muttered, Mrs. Duncan did not entirely catch them, and she went away to her own room, leaving Dorothy to decide on her costume for herself.

CHAPTER 11: FLIRTATION

GLANCING from her window, Dorothy saw Mabel and Leila strolling across the lawn deeply engrossed in conversation.

"Perhaps they've heard something!" she said to herself. "I'll get dressed early and go down."

Had she heard what the two were saying, she might not have cared to go down so soon, for they were talking of her.

"She's a dear," said Leila, "and I hate to realize what a little flirt she is."

"She's so pretty, she can't help it," said Mabel.

"But she ought to have a little regard for the proprieties."

"Why, what has she done very dreadful?"

"Oh, it isn't so very dreadful, but it doesn't look well."

"What is it? Tell me."

"Well, don't you breathe it, but last night, awfully late, I saw her creeping slyly downstairs."

"Why, she was in my room until we went to bed," and Leila looked uninterested.

"Oh, I mean later than that. It was almost two o'clock."

"What!"

"Yes, it was. There was a window shade flapping in the hall, and it kept me awake, and I got up to fix it, and I saw Dorothy in one of those lovely negligees of hers, moving along the wall toward the stairs."

"Did you see her go down?"

"Yes; she had her hair in two long braids and a rosebuddy little cap on."

"What was she going down for?"

"I don't know, I'm sure. To flirt with somebody, I suppose. I didn't tell Fred, he hates anything like eavesdropping, and I wasn't;—I just saw her by the merest chance."

"I wonder who was down there," said Leila thoughtfully.

"Probably that Mr. Chapin. He's wild over Dorothy."

"Who isn't? She has more charm than any girl I ever saw."

"Who says she hasn't? I know how pretty and attractive she is. But that doesn't excuse friskiness like that. She oughtn't to do it."

"Perhaps she went down for water, or to get a book, or something."

"Perhaps she didn't! You know the appointments of this house better than that! And she wasn't in a kimono. It was one of those white, lacy Parisian boudoir robes of hers, with a bunch of that scarlet sage she's always wearing, stuck in her belt. Oh, she was on an escapade all right!"

"A harmless one, I'm sure. Maybe she was going to see Justin."

"More likely Chapin. I tell you she's in love with him."

"I don't think so."

"Then you can't read signs. You watch them to-night. Well, it's dressing time. I suppose those Philadelphia men will come soon. And I do hope Justin will show up. I haven't the least fear about him, have you?"

"I don't know whether I have or I haven't," and Leila looked anxious. "It's awfully queer,— and yet I can't think there's anything wrong. Goodness, there's Dorothy, all dressed. Doesn't she look lovely!"

And Dorothy did. The exquisite gown of rose satin and silver tulle draped her dainty figure in a soft silhouette, and her rounded babyish arms and neck needed no jewel or ornament to accent their loveliness.

She paused for a bit of gay banter with the two, and then, as they went on, she turned toward the South

Terrace, half hoping she'd find Ernest Chapin there. For wilful Dorothy had not the slightest intention of obeying her mother's injunctions regarding that young man.

Chapin, was not there, but Campbell Crosby was. He stood leaning against the terrace rail, with folded arms, looking out across the ravine. Dorothy went softly up to him, and stood by his side. As he turned and saw her, his face lighted up with a glad smile of greeting, and, taking both her hands in his, he said in a low tone, "Oh, I'm so glad to be back—with you."

It was no new thing to Dorothy Duncan to learn that a man was glad to come back to her, and she had long known that Campbell Crosby was desperately in love with her. But the little coquette had truly given her whole heart to Ernest Chapin, and since she had realized this she had no room in that really true and loyal little heart for even the shadow of any other man. But she could not change her innate spirit of coquetry, and so she flashed a meaning glance from her dark eyes to Crosby's, as she murmured, "Am I the real reason you're glad to be back?"

"Yes," said Crosby, coming a step nearer, and forcibly repressing a mad desire to take her in his arms; "and you know it, Dorothy!"

While not denying it, Dorothy assumed an expression of great gravity, and said pleadingly, "Don't look at me like that. Remember the real reason you are here—to help us find Justin. Oh, Mr. Crosby, where do you think he can be?"

"I don't care where he is," said Crosby, flinging discretion to the winds, "so long as he isn't here to forbid my looking at you."

Now, when Ernest Chapin said this sort of thing, Dorothy's heart was glad, however much she might pretend to be offended. But aside from the passing interest she felt in every man, she had no particular favor to show to Campbell Crosby. And so she frowned as she answered, "Please don't talk like that, Mr. Crosby. Do you know, I can't help thinking something has happened to Justin."

"Nonsense! He'll turn up at dinner-time, hungry as a hunter, and with a perfectly good explanation of where he's been and what he's been up to."

"Oh, do you think so!" cried Dorothy, and a great wave of relief passed over her. Somehow the assertion of this big lawyer man carried a sense of security and safety.

"It's an ill wind that blows nobody good," went on Crosby. "Gale and I have a most important case requiring our attention in Philadelphia just now, but as soon as he heard the news this morning, he decreed that we should come here at once—both of us. And you may be sure that *I* raised no objection."

The admiring look that accompanied this speech gave a lead that Dorothy followed almost unconsciously, so accustomed was she to this sort of thing.

"I'm glad you didn't object too strongly," she answered, and the swift rise and fall of her long lashes added a deeper meaning to the words than they possessed. Indeed, they didn't possess any, and Dorothy was really thinking of something else at the time, but this was her way with a man.

"Does that mean you're glad I'm here? Oh, Dorothy, let it mean that! Please do!"

Dorothy looked at him provokingly, tantalizingly. "Of course I'm glad you're here. You and Mr. Gale will help us find Justin, won't you?"

"Do leave Justin out for a moment, and think only of me."

"I will—for a moment." Dorothy leaned against the vine-clad pillar and gazed intently at the young man. There was a mocking smile in her eyes that irritated, while it fascinated, him. He returned her gaze steadily, and said in low, tense tones, "You think it's just for a moment, don't you? Well, you're going to look at me like that for the rest of your life!"

Dorothy burst into a merry laugh. Accustomed though she was to admiration, and even to sudden proposals, this calm announcement of Crosby's seemed the most audacious thing she had ever heard.

"Guess again," she said saucily. "As soon as you find Justin for me, I shall reserve all my gazes for him, and for him only."

"But suppose," began Crosby, speaking slowly and very seriously—" suppose Justin—"

"I know what you're going to say: suppose Justin never-comes back? I have begun to suppose that. I can't help it. It's very mysterious, but it must be that something has happened to him. What could it be, Mr. Crosby?"

"How should I know? He was all right when I left here yesterday. But, Dorothy, listen to me a moment. If he should never return, if you are freed from him forever, won't you let me—"

Dorothy interrupted him a little sharply. "Don't talk like that, Mr. Crosby. This is no time for such a subject."

"But the time will come, and I can wait, my beautiful Dorothy!"

Campbell Crosby was a tall man, of fine physique and bearing. And as he stood calmly looking down at little Dorothy, he gave an impression of splendid power, and the girl looked at him with a new admiration. She liked a masterful man, and, though she had never taken any special interest in Campbell Crosby, she suddenly realized that he was a worthwhile man. But then the thought of Ernest Chapin returned to her, and she knew that, compared to him, all other men were as nothing to her.

"Campbell," she said, sending a thrill through him as he heard her pronounce his name, "you mustn't talk to me like that. I forbid it!" But as the forbidding was accompanied by a snowflake of a hand laid lightly on his arm, it wasn't absolutely successful.

Crosby laid his own hand over hers. "Well, haven't I just said I won't? Or, at least,—that I will wait. Now, how do you want me to talk to you?"

"Oh, anyway, just to pass the time till the others come down."

"And I'm simply a stop-gap, am I! Very well, I'm content; but I warn you I shall make the most of my time!"

"What are you going to do?" and Dorothy looked at him provokingly.

"Hold your hand, for one thing," and Crosby clasped it in both of his. "And then, if I can get a real good chance, when no one is looking I—may— kiss—"

"Mr. Crosby!"

"—may kiss your finger tips," went on Crosby, calmly.

"Oh!" and naughty Dorothy looked purposely disappointed. She smiled at him, and the red lips so near his own, and the soft faint perfume of her hair made his senses reel, and catching her in his arms he kissed her madly, and then held her off at arms' length.

"There!" he said, lightly, "that's what little girls get when they come too near!"

"Was I too near?" and Dorothy put up the face of a rebuked cherub.

"Dorothy, stop! I can't stand it! Have you no mercy, child? But some day, you shall be all my very own! You say this is no time to tell you this, and so I will wait; but, the time will come, my little love. When,—when Justin returns, I shall tell him you are mine,—not his!"

"Oh, I don't think so, Mr. Crosby," and Dorothy shrugged her dimpled shoulders as she turned away.

"A lady's consent is thought to be necessary to such an arrangement."

"Not for me," and Crosby smiled gaily; "I'm a Cave Man, and I shall carry off the lady I want, regardless of her wishes."

Crosby stood with folded arms, looking very big and handsome. Of magnificent physique, and in splendid condition, he seemed quite capable of picking up a maiden and running away with her.

The idea amused Dorothy. "When Cave Men carry off little girls," she said, "do they throw them over their shoulders,—or just grabble them up under their arms?"

Crosby considered. "There are various technical methods," he said; "if it's a very big man and a very little girl, as in this case, he just—well, I'll show you "

"No, don't!" cried Dorothy; "here comes Mrs. Crane!"

"Some other time, then," murmured Crosby, and turned to greet Mabel.

"I'm so glad you came, dear," said Dorothy; "I've entertained Mr. Crosby to the very limit of my powers. He's bored to death with me; so you take him in charge while I run and play with Mr. Gale. Hello, Emory! Here's me!"

Others came then, and soon there were several groups, all trying to avoid the subject of Arnold's disappearance, but all coming back to it sooner or later.

Mabel Crane did not hesitate. "Mr. Crosby," she said, at once, "they tell me you know all about this place. Now I want to ask you something. Is there any secret passage of any kind in this old house?"

"Secret passage! What do you mean?"

"Why, I'm determined to find Justin, myself, if possible. Now, they all say he couldn't have gotten out of this house last night. But if there is a secret passage that no one knows about, of course he could have gone out that way. And they said that you would know if there was one."

"Who said that?" asked Crosby.

"Why, I don't know—Miss Wadsworth, I think. At any rate, they all agreed that if any such thing exists, you would be likely to know about it."

"Of course I should. I know every nook and corner of this house, both the old original structure and the modern additions. You see, I always spent my summers here as a boy, and Justin and I were everlastingly exploring the place. No, there is no secret passage. Those things are built in mediaeval castles, or sometimes in old English mansions, but I fancy there are not many in America. At any rate, there are no sliding panels or staircases in the wall at White Birches. Of that I'm positive."

"I thought there couldn't be," said Mabel, "or we should have heard of it before. But then, where is Justin, and how did he get out of the house?"

Crosby passed his hand wearily across his brow. "Mrs. Crane," he said, "I fear that question will be asked many times before it is answered. Of course, my own theory—"

Some of the others joined them just then, and as Mabel took little interest in theories, when she wanted to learn facts, she did not ask Crosby to finish his sentence.

Conversation at dinner touched more or less upon the subject of the mystery, but the talk was not general, and each one merely exchanged views with his neighbor. The vacant chair at the head of the table cast an atmosphere of gloom over the diners. Little was eaten, and all were glad when Miss Wadsworth gave the signal to rise.

Nor was it long before the men drifted into the library, where the women sat awaiting them.

"It seems to me," began Miss Wadsworth," that the time has come to do something more definite in our search for Justin. We have asked Mr. Gale and Mr. Crosby, as lawyers, to advise us, but I think that we must employ the services of some professional."

"You mean a detective?" asked Fred Crane. "I thought you seriously objected to that."

"I did at first; but since I've talked with Mr. Gale I'm more reconciled to the idea."

"I think the matter is a very grave one," said Emory Gale, tacitly assuming an attitude of leading the discussion, somewhat to the discomfiture of Mr. Crane, who himself coveted that position. "We have few facts to work upon," continued Gale, "but they are startling ones and apparently inexplicable. We are convinced that the extreme efficacy of the burglar-alarm prevented Arnold from leaving the house; and yet he is not to be found in the house. Of course I am assuming that the search of the house has been thorough, as I am informed it has been. There has been suggestion of a secret panel leading to a concealed staircase or passage through the wall, but this idea seems to me fanciful. Had there been such a thing, we doubtless would have known of it, for Arnold was fond of exhibiting such features of the house as were peculiar or interesting. Crosby, you know the house well. Does it contain any secret doors or passages?"

"It does not," replied Crosby. "As boys, Justin and I explored every part of the estate, both house and grounds, and no such secret passage exists.'"

"Then we may eliminate that theory," went on Gale; "and so we are again confronted by a blank wall of seeming contradictions. Arnold is not in the house—yet he could not get out of the house. But there must be an explanation, and, speaking theoretically, I can find but two possible ones. Either he left the house by the assistance or connivance of some one inside its walls, or else he had a means of exit unknown to others."

Though these suggestions were somewhat veiled, every one understood that what Gale really meant was that he suspected that someone in the house, either guest or servant, knew more than had been told.

But without enlarging on this point, the speaker went on: "However, if he did leave the house, by any means whatever, I cannot think it possible that he left the grounds; the only exit being the great gate, and no human being could go out through that and fasten its chains and bolts again on the inside. Nor could he get over the absolutely unscalable wall. So without advancing it as a theory exactly, I can't help a vague impression that Arnold might have gone for a walk in the grounds after midnight, and fallen by accident into some deep pool or well. I know this sounds somewhat implausible, but I can't think of anything else that will be a rational explanation of the man's disappearance. And that he went away intending to mystify us all, I shall never believe. So my advice, since it has been asked, is to put the matter into professional hands. I myself should inform the police, but Miss Wadsworth and Mrs. Duncan naturally shrink from giving the affair so much publicity. So, to my mind, the next best plan is to send at once for the best detective from the Central Office."

"I quite agree with you," observed Mr. Crane.

"I'm sure it is a case for a detective, but I warn you he will find it hard to discover any clues. Mrs. Crane and I went over the grounds carefully this afternoon, and we found no footprints, nor any suggestive indications of any sort."

Mr. Crane spoke as if he were giving information of vast importance, but Gale did not seem especially impressed. "One could hardly expect to find footprints in this weather," he said. "It is clear and cold and the ground is hard. Of course the gravel walks would show no footprints, nor the stone pavements. I think a detective will scarcely depend upon clues of that sort—though I must admit I can't see what he will find to depend on. To me, the affair is entirely mysterious, unless there has been foul play of some sort."

This was the first time foul play had been definitely mentioned, and everybody started at the idea.

Dorothy threw herself into her mother's arms and began to cry. Leila Duane and Mabel Crane were whispering together earnestly, while Miss Wadsworth sat bolt upright, her face turning ashy white at the suggestion.

The men, too, all looked disturbed at the thought. All modern, up-to-date men of the world, their minds immediately jumped to thoughts of what it would mean if there were really tragedy, possibly crime, and the unpleasant details of public exposure.

Mr. Crane, perhaps, had thought of this before, for he nodded his head gravely, with an expression of superior sagacity; but the others seemed appalled, and sat quiet, but deeply thoughtful.

"I've no wish to alarm you unnecessarily," pursued Gale, "but I am so firmly convinced that it is foreign to Mr. Arnold's nature to do anything erratic or purposely mysterious, that I am forced to the conclusion, or rather to the suspicion, of wrong-doing on the part of—someone else."

"But how—but who—" began Miss Abby, helplessly.

"I don't know," said Gale; "I have no theory, not even an idea, further than this: if Mr. Arnold is kept unwillingly away from home, it is either by accident or force. If accident, we shall probably learn of it in a short time. If force, it is our imperative duty to find him. We have no idea which way to turn or what way to look, therefore, I advise a clever and capable detective. Do not think, Miss Wadsworth, there is anything sinister or fearful about a detective. He is perhaps no cleverer or wiser than the men gathered here, but his training and experience give him advantages that other citizens do not possess. Employing a detective by no means implies a fear of tragedy or disaster; it is merely the rational way to go about the solution of what we must admit has become a real mystery. And, as I have said, if there is no real mystery, if Mr. Arnold turns up safe and sound and laughs at our fears, then there is no harm done. But to neglect or delay our efforts, if they are necessary, is criminal on our part. I don't want to dictate, but you called us over here to advise you, and the advice I have just given, is, I am sure, the opinion of my partner also. Isn't it, Crosby?"

"Certainly," and Campbell Crosby spoke with decision. "I think there is nothing else to do, but act as you have suggested, Gale. I naturally wish the affair might be kept as quiet as possible, for when my cousin appears, as it is my belief he soon will, it would be best to have as little notoriety about it all as possible."

Fred Crane was the only one who raised a definite objection. "I think," he began, "it is premature to call in a detective now. What can he do, but pry round and investigate, and that we can do ourselves. I am of a detective turn of mind, myself, and I am glad to offer my services in the matter. While not precisely a Sherlock Holmes, I have a strong deductive faculty, and I feel sure I could do all that a professional could accomplish, the more so that I have a personal interest in the matter, which he could not have."

"There's something in that," said Campbell Crosby, thoughtfully; "often an amateur succeeds because of his personal note of determination, where a professional is actuated only by thought of reward."

Emory Gale looked annoyed. "Of course you must all do as you choose," he said. "Miss Wadsworth, I look to you for orders. I am Mr. Arnold's lawyer, and in his absence I defer to your wishes. What do you think about the matter of engaging a detective?"

Miss Abby fidgeted. "I don't know," she said finally; "at first I was terribly opposed to such a thing. But now I feel we ought to get one. It is presentiment or premonition or something of that sort, perhaps, but I do feel there's something wrong about Justin's absence. However, I am not the only one to be consulted. As Justin's promised wife and as future mistress of this place, I think Dorothy's wishes should be considered. What do you think, dear?"

"Oh, don't ask me!" cried Dorothy, in an agonized voice; "not me, of all people!"

"Why not, dear?" said her mother, gently.

"Come, Dorothy, darling, don't act like that. You have a certain responsibility, you must rise to meet it."

"Oh, I can't! I can't! Don't ask me,—ask anyone else— anyone!"

CHAPTER 12: A CHECK STUB

AND so as Miss Wadsworth seemed to be the only one to decide the question, she did so by quietly directing that a professional detective be engaged.

"Don't think I don't appreciate your offer," she said to Fred Crane; "but with all the willingness in the world, I don't think you could do the work of a trained detective. And anyway, you can both work together. No doubt the Central Office man will be glad of your sympathetic interest and assistance."

Crane was not overly pleased at this, but he couldn't very well insist, so he agreed to do all he could to help, vowing to himself that he would accomplish some wonderful sleuthing that would make the real detective "sit up and take notice."

As there was no reason for delay and there might be reason for immediate action, Gale telephoned at once to the Central Office for a first-class detective. He was advised that James Wheeler would be sent the next morning and that Mr. Wheeler was one of the best and cleverest men on the force.

"I think he might have come to-night," said Miss Abby; "if anything dreadful has happened to Justin, every hour counts."

"He couldn't do anything to-night," Crosby assured her. "I've heard of Wheeler, he's a very clever man, and I've no doubt when he comes he will solve the mystery."

"And perhaps it will be but a simple solution," said Leila Duane, hopefully, "and perhaps there isn't any dreadfulness about it at all."

"Then where's Justin?" demanded Dorothy, looking up with tearful eyes, from her mother's embrace.

"We don't know yet, dear," returned Mrs. Duncan, gently; "we hope Mr. Wheeler will find out."

"Meantime, let us be doing something by way of investigation," said Gale, who was of an impatient nature. "What do you say, Miss Wadsworth, do you think I'm justified in looking through the papers in Arnold's desk or safe? I don't want to intrude, but mightn't we learn something, perhaps, that way?"

Miss Abby considered. "As his lawyer, Mr. Gale, I think you have a perfect right to look over his papers. As confidential secretary, Mr. Chapin also has a right. So if you and Mr. Crosby and Mr. Chapin choose to go over his business papers, I'm sure I have no objections."

The three men went off on their errand, and if Mr. Crane felt any chagrin at not being asked to accompany them, he successfully concealed it. Following Ernest Chapin, Gale and Crosby soon found themselves in the pleasant room which Justin Arnold used as his business office, though its elaborate appointments made such a name seen inappropriate.

Everything was in perfect order, for Arnold was methodical and systematic in all his ways, and his secretary was no less so.

With professional rapidity, Gale and Crosby ran through the desk. There was nothing in any of the business papers, letters, or books of memoranda to indicate anything unusual or mysterious in the life or habits of Justin Arnold.

At the request of the lawyers, Ernest Chapin opened the great safe, which was built into the wall, and which was of modern and elaborate device. Here too everything was in order. Certain bonds and deeds were there, and memoranda told of others that were in banks or safety deposit vaults.

The extent of their client's wealth was a slight surprise to both Gale and Crosby, for though they had known Arnold to be a rich man, they did not know the extent of his fortune. Emory Gale gave a low whistle as he read some of the statements, but Crosby said frankly, "By George! I didn't know old Justin had such a lot of money!"

"His investments for many years have turned out very favorably," said Ernest Chapin, but he spoke in a dull, hard voice, and with a preoccupied air, as if thinking of other matters.

"Well, there's certainly nothing here by way of a clue to steer us in any direction," remarked Gale; "but I'm glad, Crosby, that we went through these papers ourselves. Now there's no need of that detective prying into them. We can assure him that there's absolutely nothing to be found that would throw any light on Justin's disappearance."

"That's so," agreed Crosby. "Hello, Gale, here's his private check-book. I suppose we ought to look through that, though it does seem intrusive."

"Is it necessary?" asked Ernest Chapin, making a half-involuntary movement, as if to take the book.

Campbell Crosby looked at him curiously. A flush had risen to Chapin's temples, and a slight quiver in his voice showed an agitation he was striving hard to control.

Crosby noted this, and said coolly, "Why, yes, I think it is necessary." So saying, he opened the book and ran over the stubs. They seemed innocent enough, and suggested nothing mysterious. The names on the stubs were mostly such firms as tailors or hatters, with here and there a friend's name or that of a charitable organization. About to return it to its place, Crosby caught sight of the last entry, and he stared at it in astonishment. "Why, Chapin, this last stub is for a check made out to you, for five thousand dollars!" he said.

"Yes?" said Chapin, in a faint voice, while his face went white. "Is it?"

"Is it," went on Crosby; "and, what's more, it's dated to-day. To-day, October seventh! Have you seen Arnold to-day?"

"N-no," stammered Chapin; "well, that is, not exactly to-day."

"What nonsense are you talking?" demanded Gale. "What do you mean by 'not exactly to-day'?

Why did Arnold give you a check for five thousand dollars? You have seen him to-day? Where is he?"

This rapid fire of angry questions seemed to restore Chapin's self-possession, and he answered coldly, "I resent the tone you use, Mr. Gale, and I refuse to answer questions couched in such language. As Mr. Arnold's secretary, and in his confidence, I refuse to discuss any expenditures he may have made, whether to myself or anyone else."

"But, man alive," went on Gale, in amazement, "don't take that attitude! Don't array yourself against us! Are we not all working for the same end? Are we not all interested in finding Arnold? And if you have seen him to-day, and this check is dated to-day, you must tell us!"

"You have no right to say 'must' to me, Mr. Gale."

"Oh, don't quibble about words," said Crosby.

"Explain it, Chapin, as man to man. Have you the check that was torn from that stub?"

"Of course I have. Mr. Arnold gave it to me."

"When?"

"I must ask what right you gentlemen have to cross-question me. Am I on trial?"

"You are not," said Gale coldly; "but if you persist in showing such strong disinclination to answer questions bearing directly on the business in hand, I am forced to think you ought to be on trial. I ask you in a friendly manner to explain the peculiar circumstance of your receiving a large check from Justin Arnold to-day, when nobody else knows where the man is."

Chapin looked both injured and sullen. "The check is of a private and personal nature," he said, at last. "Mr. Arnold gave it to me last night, here in this office. As it was after midnight when he drew the check, of course he dated it to-day. As I have already declared, I left Mr.

Arnold here last night at about half-past twelve. That's what I meant by saying I hadn't exactly seen him to-day. Of course, last night after midnight was literally to-day, and it was before Mr. Arnold's mysterious disappearance."

Emory Gale looked perturbed and a little suspicious. Campbell Crosby looked frankly amazed.

It might all be exactly as Chapin had said, and Justin Arnold might have had ample reasons for presenting his secretary with a sum of money probably equal to his year's salary; but it was a peculiar coincidence that the man should disappear immediately afterward. If Chapin had treated it lightly, and explained why he received so large a sum at one time, and whether or not it was by way of salary, the lawyers would have thought little of it. But when the secretary was so evidently rattled, so unwilling to explain matters, and so clearly annoyed at being questioned, it was but natural for the two lawyers to feel some curiosity concerning the occurrence. However, Emory Gale, who was perhaps more far-sighted than his junior partner, said calmly, "You're right, Mr. Chapin; it isn't exactly in our province to question you. Whatever conclusions we may draw from the examination of the papers are of course our own affairs, as your relations with your employer are yours."

Though spoken quietly, Mr. Gale's words seemed to have a deeper meaning than was apparent on the surface, and the pallor that overspread Ernest Chapin's face proved that he realized this. Leaving the agitated secretary with the check-book in his hand, and the safe open beside him, Mr. Gale and Mr. Crosby walked away.

"Deucedly queer development!" said Crosby; and Gale returned, "It's more than that. To my mind, it implicates Chapin pretty deeply in the matter. But it isn't up to us to probe the case. When the detective comes to-morrow, he can do that. Any way, Chapin can't run away as long as this place is guarded like a fortress. I wonder if they'll turn on their precious burglar-alarm to-night."

"Of course they will. Old Driggs always did it when Justin was away, so, naturally, he'll attend to it."

It was early the next morning that Dorothy came downstairs. That is, it was early for her to make an appearance, though the other members of the household had already assembled. But the girl was too anxious to learn if there were any news to remain in her room as usual.

Absolutely nothing had been discovered concerning Arnold, and breakfast was eaten in an atmosphere of almost gloomy silence. Now and then someone would endeavor to make a cheerful remark, but it was not followed up in the same spirit.

After breakfast, Dorothy strolled out to the terrace, where she was immediately joined by Crosby and Chapin. It was not a congenial trio, but Dorothy was accustomed to managing men who were at odds with each other, and she found no difficulty in keeping them both in her company.

"Just think," she said, "of not knowing anything about where Justin may be! Why, he might be drowned, or anything!"

"I think we ought to have the pools dragged," said Ernest Chapin, and as he spoke directly to Dorothy, he evaded Crosby's searching glance.

"I think so, too," agreed the girl; "for I think we ought to do everything that could possibly be of any use. But I can't seem to imagine Justin walking out in the middle of the night, and falling into one of his own pools."

"They're very deep," said Crosby.

"I know they are; that black one under the willows makes me shiver to look at it; and that dark one down in that deepest ravine is positively uncanny!"

Leila and Gale strolled past the group, saying they were going around the grounds to hunt for clues.

Crosby looked after them, a little amusedly. "They won't see any clues, if they stumble over them!" he said.

"They don't know there's anything in this world but each other."

"That's so," said Dorothy; "aren't they desperately in love? It must be beautiful to-be in love like that!"

It was almost unthinkingly that Dorothy spoke thus out of the fulness of her heart. Though she did love Chapin, she had no intention of confessing it or even letting it be suspected; for Ernest Chapin was a poor man, and Dorothy Duncan was a girl who fully intended to marry money.

But the two men who listened to this, speech were both deeply in love with her, and each determined then and there that she should yet be desperately in love with him. How this desirable state of things was to be brought about, neither knew, but each was none the less positive in his intention. A little later, Miss Wadsworth claimed Crosby's attention, and Ernest Chapin was left alone with Dorothy.

"Listen to me," he said, without preamble. "That detective is coming at ten o'clock, and I want to remind you, once more, to say nothing about Arnold's seeing us on the balcony together. The detective will question you, but no good can possibly come of your telling of that scene, and it might result in harm."

"Well, I won't; but I want you to tell me what Justin said to you after I left you."

"Nothing of any importance—as I told you before."

"Was he angry?"

"Yes, he was." And then, as if on a sudden impulse, Chapin whispered earnestly to the girl, "Dorothy, darling, if you'll only admit you love me—I know you do—I'll tell you everything about it. What Arnold said, and all that happened. And you can confide in me, too—"

Dorothy's eyes opened wide, "Ernest, you don't mean that you know anything about Justin's going away!"

"I'll tell you nothing," he returned doggedly, "until you tell me what I ask. Tell me, dear."

Dorothy looked at him with a gentle tenderness.

"Ernest," she sai'd softly, "this isn't the time or place or such a question."

"Yes, it is, darling. There couldn't be a more beautiful place than this terrace, with the bright sunshine and blue sky above, and no one near to overhear us. Answer me, Dorothy. Crown my happiness of loving you, by your dear confession that you love me."

Dorothy was strongly tempted to tell this man that she did love him. She longed to see his eyes light up with the happiness that she knew such an admission would bring. Then her glance roved out over the wide domain spread out before her: the beautiful terrace on which they stood, and the great mansion behind them. Could she give up all this for her love of Ernest Chapin? It didn't seem to her that she could. Then, at the intrusion of a sudden thought, she ignored her lover's pleading, and said, "As Justin's secretary, Mr. Chapin, of course you know all about his business matters. If he should —if he should never come back, who would own White Birches?"

"I am not quite sure. If Mr. Arnold made no will, his whole estate will go to Campbell Crosby; but if he made a will—and I'm quite sure he did, though I've never seen it—of course the disposition of his fortune will be in accordance with that. I do know that he intended to make a will before his marriage, leaving everything to you, but whether he has done so or not, I'm not sure."

"His lawyers will know, won't they?"

"Yes; unless he made merely a private memorandum, which, if signed, will be valid. But, Dorothy, you talk as if he were dead! And, oh, child, if he is, if he should be, you don't mean,—you can't mean, that you want to know who inherits White Birches —to know where to turn your affections next!"

Dorothy had the grace to look ashamed of herself, and, moved by Chapin's evident misery, she said softly, "If Justin never returns, there is only one place for my affections."

The look she gave Chapin left no doubt of her meaning, and, taking both her hands in his, he said, "Oh, darling, you've admitted it at last! You make me so happy, dear, and, whether Arnold returns or not, he shall never claim you after that admission!"

"Oh, yes, he will! I'm bound to him, and of course he will return, and of course I shall marry him. But now tell me what he said to you. You promised you would."

"He wasn't at all nice, dear. He accused me of being a traitor to him, and of acting dishonorably in loving the girl he was engaged to."

"Well, it isn't very honorable, is it?"

"All's fair in love and war. And, anyway, if I could win you only through dishonor, I would pause at no crime!"

"Oh, Ernest, what a dreadful speech! Don't say such things. You make me shiver!"

"But it's true, Dorothy: I would hesitate at nothing, if you were the reward."

Just then Gale and Leila returned from a walk through the grounds, and though Dorothy greeted them casually, as if her conversation with Chapin were most unimportant, the man could not so easily shake off a feeling of self-consciousness. To hide it, he became glum and taciturn, responding in monosyllables, when he spoke at all.

"We didn't find any clues around the place," said Leila. "Now we're going to look through the house. Mr. Gale and I have discovered that we both have the 'detective instinct,' and we're working together on this case." It was clear to the most incurious observer that Gale and Leila were more interested in their discoveries about each other than in their "case," but Dorothy had affairs of her own on her mind, and Chapin was uninterested, so the two amateur detectives passed on into the house to continue their search.

In a few moments Leila came running back.

"Dorothy," she cried, "did you take a green sofa pillow from the couch in the living-room? The one embroidered in gold thread?"

"No, Leila, I haven't seen it. Why should I take a sofa-cushion from its place?"

"Well, it's gone; and nobody knows anything about it, and we think it is a clue!"

"Oh, Leila, how ridiculous! How could a missing sofa-pillow be a clue? Probably one of the maids took it to mend it, or something."

"No," and Leila spoke positively; "it didn't need mending. It was a new one, and it was so pretty that I was going to copy the embroidery. That's the way I happened to miss it. It's gone, and nobody knows anything about it!"

"It does seem queer," said Gale, who had followed Leila out.

"Fiddlesticks!" said Dorothy. "If you two people weren't so anxious to make anything serve as a clue, you'd know that that sofa-pillow would turn up somewhere. Do you suppose Justin kidnapped it and took it away, or do you suppose a burglar came in through a keyhole, purposely to get it?"

Ernest Chaplin looked thoughtful. "Did it have a thick gold cord all round it, and tassels at one corner?" he asked.

"Yes," answered Leila eagerly. "Did you take it away, Mr. Chapin?"

"No," and Ernest Chapin spoke slowly; "I remember having seen it, that is all."

Leila and Gale went away to make further search for the sofa-pillow, and Chapin fell into a brown study, from which even Dorothy's chatter failed to rouse him.

CHAPTER 13: THE DETECTIVE

"I KNOW," said Leila, thoughtfully, her pretty blonde head on one side, "that it seems silly to Dorothy, but I do believe that sofa-pillow has something to do with the mystery."

"I'm sure it has," said Gale, who was approaching that point where if Leila had said the phase of the moon was responsible for Arnold's disappearance, he would have agreed with her. "But for the life of me, I can't see how."

"Nor I," and Leila's straight brows contracted as she puzzled over the matter. "But you know, Mr. Gale, it is queer that it should get away so suddenly, and, too, detectives always find out things from some such strange incident as that. When Mr. Wheeler comes, I've no doubt he'll consider it a matter of importance, but I want to deduce for myself what it means."

But Leila couldn't get any inkling of the sofacushion's present whereabouts, nor could she form any theory of how it could possibly be connected with Justin's absence.

"It's utterly absurd, Leila," said Fred Crane, "to imagine a sofa-pillow as a clue! What part could it play in the mystery? You don't suppose Justin took it with him?"

"No; of course he wouldn't do that. And yet, where is it? It was here on Monday, for I was matching its colors to make one like it. I've asked the housekeeper and the servants."

"What did they say?" asked Crane, not much interested.

"Only Mrs. Garson and the parlor-maid remembered it at all. And they said they knew nothing about it."

"Perhaps the parlor-maid stole it," volunteered Gale. "You say it was a valuable one."

"Not valuable," corrected Leila, "but especially pretty. But Polly wouldn't steal it. She seems a nice girl. Maybe she took it to copy it, and was afraid to own up."

"That's probably it," said Crane. "But it can't possibly be connected with Justin Arnold in any way."

The three were still discussing the sofa-cushion when Mr. Wheeler arrived. The entire household assembled in the living-room to meet him.

While by no means a fine-looking or distinguished man, James Wheeler gave an impression of capability. Rather short and of stocky build, his alert air and quick movements invested him with a degree of importance, and his shrewd eyes betokened an incisive intelligence and a good sense of values. He was plain and straightforward in his methods. No sly and subtle manoeuvring for him. Plain facts, and logical deductions therefrom, constituted his stock-in-trade. His manner was a trifle pompous, as fitted his calling, but he was courteous and deferential, and liked quick action when once he set about his business.

He seated himself in a large chair at one end of the long room, and seemed to take a hasty mental stock of the people grouped about before he spoke at all. He glanced appraisingly at Miss Wadsworth, but as that lady was exceedingly nervous and almost hysterical, the detective looked further for a nominal head of the house.

Fred Crane read his thoughts and volunteered:

"Mr. Wheeler, I daresay you want someone to give you the principal facts of the matter in hand, and I will do so. While by no means a detective in the technical sense of the term, I am by nature of a reasoning mind, and I've no doubt I can tell you the salient features more concisely than some of the others present."

Wheeler looked at him. "Thank you, sir," he said, "but I'll not trouble you. I may be peculiar, but I prefer to get at the facts in my own way. Of course, I know that Mr. Arnold has mysteriously been absent since Monday night, or rather Tuesday morning. For he may not have left the house until after daylight. It is now Wednesday morning, and it seems desirable to endeavor to learn where he may be. I will, if you please, address my inquiries to one or another as I may be inclined, but if anyone knows of any important fact I trust he will state it when the occasion calls for it."

Though the confidential secretary was perhaps the best informed as to his employer's habits and customs, yet a glance at Chapin's gloomy and forbidding face caused the detective to look in another direction. Mr. Crane, he deemed too officious and too anxious to give information, so he settled on the firm of lawyers, and chose Gale, as being the senior member.

Mr. Wheeler did not say that he had thus made an intentional selection, nor did it take him more than a moment to make up his mind. With a quiet manner, that somehow held the rest listening in silence, he asked some questions of Emory Gale. In a few moments he was in possession of the main facts of the case as known.

"Do you think Mr. Arnold could have been drowned?" he asked abruptly.

"No," replied Gale; "I don't think that."

"Do you think he is, for any reason, hiding on purpose?"

"I do not," said Gale decidedly.

"He is not, then, a man who would do such a thing, say, as a practical joke?"

"Decidedly not!" said Gale emphatically.

Wheeler nodded his head. "I understand," he proceeded, "that Mr. Arnold was more or less in the habit of walking in his grounds at night. I mean, when he had no guests, he was given to prowling about among the trees."

"That is true," volunteered Miss Wadsworth, as Gale seemed a little uncertain on this point.

"When he took such walks, did he usually wear hat and overcoat?"

"Yes," replied Miss Abby; "a coat according to the weather, but always a hat. Justin never went out without a hat."

Remembering his fairly well advanced state of baldness, no one was surprised at this.

"Then," went on Mr. Wheeler, "have you investigated his wardrobe, and learned what hat and coat are missing?"

No one had thought to do this, and the valet was summoned to answer questions.

"Peters," said Mr. Wheeler, "do you know all the hats and coats in Mr. Arnold's possession?"

"Certainly, sir," said Peters, with the respectful assurance of the well-trained servant. "And could you tell if any were missing?"

"Yes, sir."

"And have you made any search?"

"Not to say, sir, exactly a search, but I couldn't help noticing that all Mr. Arnold's hats and top-coats are in their places, and I wondered, sir, what he might have worn on his head when he went away."

"You're positive, Peters, that there is no hat or overcoat missing?"

"I'm positive, sir."

"Has any guest present, or any of the servants, missed a hat or a cap?"

Investigation soon proved that nobody had missed any.

"Mr. Arnold was in evening dress when last seen?"

"Yes," answered Miss Abby; "Justin was always in evening dress after six o'clock. He was most punctilious in that respect, like his father before him."

"And that suit of evening clothes is not in his wardrobe, Peters?"

"No, sir."

"Nor his shoes, nor tie, nor any of the garments that he wore the last time you assisted at his toilet?"

"No, sir; they are all missing from his wardrobe."

"And no other garments are missing?"

"No, sir."

"Then, we are justified in concluding," said Mr. Wheeler, turning to the assembly, "that wherever Mr. Arnold may have gone, he wore the suit of clothes he had on during the evening of his disappearance, and he added no hat or outer garment.

This, in addition to the fact that he could not get out of this carefully protected house, leads me to conclude that he is still in the house. Yes, I know you have searched thoroughly, but you must have overlooked his hiding-place. It is extremely improbable that, even if Mr. Arnold could have left the house unseen, any emergency would have caused him to go bareheaded. But before I proceed to work in accordance with my own theory, I will ask if anyone has any suggestion to offer, or any information, however slight, to give that could throw light on the matter."

"It is not exactly information," said Fred Crane, "but it is a point to remember, perhaps, that Mr. Arnold would not voluntarily go away from home in evening clothes, without taking proper garments to wear on his return. Had he gone anywhere voluntarily, he would have changed or he would have carried a bag."

"Why do you say 'voluntarily,' Mr. Crane?" asked Wheeler. "Do you mean to imply Mr. Arnold could have been forced to leave his home?"

"It is merely a suggestion," and Crane looked a little important at having gained the detective's attention, "but I must say it seems impossible,"

"Of course it's impossible!" said Campbell Crosby. "Arnold couldn't get out of this locked-up house or grounds alone, much less with someone else. Malony would have known, too, if any stranger had arrived by night."

"As there are few possibilities to consider, we have to discuss impossibilities," said Crane, a little chagrined at Crosby's manner.

"Not impossibilities," said Wheeler, "but perhaps great improbabilities. The case is baffling in its very limitations. There have been no clues of any sort found, I suppose?"

"Mr. Wheeler," said Leila Duane, a little diffidently, "it may be of no importance, but I discovered this morning that a sofa-pillow was missing from the couch in this room. It was here, I am sure, day before yesterday, and now it is gone. I have questioned the servants, and no one knows anything about it."

There were half a dozen sofa pillows still on the broad-seated divan, and the detective looked slightly amused, as if one pillow more or less could really have no bearing on the case in hand.

"It may seem trivial," observed Gale, moved by a desire to lend importance to Leila's suggestion, if possible, "but you must admit, Mr. Wheeler, that a sofa-pillow couldn't get away of itself."

"No," agreed the detective gravely; "but I cannot think, Mr. Gale, that its disappearance is in any way a clue to the disappearance of Mr. Arnold. Unless he were demented, which I am informed he is not, he would scarcely go out into the night with a sofa-pillow tied on his head."

Leila looked a little chagrined at this summary dismissal of what she had fondly considered a clue; or, at least, a mysterious circumstance which might have a bearing on the greater mystery. But Mr. Wheeler made no further reference to the green sofa-pillow. He said, thoughtfully, "Who is the last one known to have seen Mr. Arnold on Monday night?"

Fred Crane, the irrepressible, spoke up. "Mr. Chapin and I were with him later than anyone else. We had been with him in the smoking-room for a short time after the ladies had retired; and about half-past twelve Mr. Chapin and myself bade Mr. Arnold good-night and went upstairs, leaving him in the smoking-room. Didn't we, Chapin?"

Ernest Chapin lifted a haggard face. "Yes," he said in low tones.

"And no one here present saw Mr. Arnold after that?" inquired the detective, his sharp eyes darting from one to another.

Nobody spoke. After a moment's silence, Mabel Crane looked at Dorothy. But the girl's face was turned away, as she sat close to her mother's side on the sofa. Then Mabel looked at Leila. But the glance was not returned. Leila kept her head resolutely turned, and stared steadfastly at a picture across the room. Mabel looked uncertain. Clearly, Dorothy had no intention of telling of her nocturnal trip downstairs that night, and Leila also was determined not to remember it.

"You look disturbed, Mrs. Crane," said the quick-sighted detective. "Did you see anything of Mr. Arnold that night?" Did you hear him on the stairs or in the halls?"

"No,—oh, no!" and Mabel shook her head.

"You did not see him strolling in the garden, or hear any doors or windows opened?"

"No, no, indeed!"

"Why are you so emphatic about it?"

Mr. Wheeler's quiet voice did not seem intrusive or overcurious, he seemed to be merely pursuing his proper course, but Mabel became so agitated that she rose and left the room. Her husband looked after her, but did not follow. "She'll return shortly," he said; "poor girl, she's very emotional, and a scene like this gets on her nerves."

And then Leila stole a glance at Dorothy. The girl was as white as death, but she was not heeding either Leila or Mabel. Her eyes were fixed on the face of the detective, and she seemed terrified yet fascinated. She looked like one in a dream or trance, and seemed to be breathlessly waiting for the next move.

Mr. Wheeler spent a moment or two in deep thought, and then said:

"Since Mr. Arnold could not get out, he must be in the house; and we cannot say he is not, until we have made an exhaustive search of the entire building. I cannot think the search that has already been made was sufficiently thorough. I will, therefore, in my direction of this case, request the assistance of such servants as I may desire to help me, and any of the men of the household who wish to may also accompany me. We will make a search that shall leave no foot of space unexplored."

Mr. Wheeler selected two of the footmen to assist him in this undertaking, and Mr. Crane volunteered also to accompany him.

Leila Duane declared that she would go, too, but Dorothy sat quietly by her mother's side, and said that nothing would induce her to go into those dark, dusky old attics again.

As a matter of course, therefore, Gale elected to accompany Leila, and Campbell Crosby remained in the library, hovering near Dorothy. Ernest Chapin, still looking gloomy as a thunder-cloud, also hovered near the pathetic little figure of the girl he loved.

In accordance with his chosen methods, Mr. Wheeler began his search in systematic order. Desiring to begin at the top of the house, he went first of all to the roof, and made his preliminary examinations from the outside. Although the servants showed him the way, he often skipped ahead of them, and showed agility and despatch in accomplishing his errands. Though they followed him to the roof, the others did not follow his various trips from one gable to another as he scurried over the various slopes and flats of tin or shingle.

His definite motive was to examine every possible exit from the house, no matter how improbable it might seem. He peered down chimneys, he looked in at dormer windows, he looked in at trap-doors and scuttles, jotting down in his note-book into what rooms they opened.

"What does this old scuttle open into?" he asked, as he looked down into pitch darkness beneath.

"I don't know exactly," answered a servant, "but I think it opens into a little loft over an ell which contains some of the servants' rooms."

Again the detective peered down into the darkness. "That's what it is," he said; "and I can see a door from the loft, but it seems to be nailed up.

I'll investigate it when we're inside the attics."

The man's energy was indefatigable. He left nothing unexamined, even looking down the leaderpipes and gutters. At last he expressed himself satisfied with his investigation of the roof, and they returned through the trap-door they had come up by, to the attics. These were numerous and rambling, but not one was omitted in the search. Every dark corner of every room, every cupboard under the eaves, every fireplace, was thoroughly illuminated by electric torches and exhaustively searched.

The tiny loft over the ell into which Wheeler had peered from above was found to have but one door, which was carefully nailed up; and, as could be easily seen from its dust and cobwebs, it had not been disturbed for decades, therefore it could not have been used recently as an exit.

They found absolutely no trace or even possibility of Justin Arnold's having left the house by means of a route through the attics.

CHAPTER 14: FOUND!

"Awful rubbish!" Fred Crane whispered to Leila;" fancy Justin, in his evening clothes, rambling around these musty old attics! He's too fastidious to think of such a thing! You know how he hates a speck of dust or dirt."

"I know," said Leila; "but I suppose Mr. Wheeler must be theorizing that Justin was escaping from somebody or something."

"Nonsense! don't be melodramatic. What could he be fleeing from?"

"I don't know, I'm sure. If we knew that, we could soon solve the mystery."

"I say," began Crane, addressing the detective, "this is all useless, you know. Arnold simply couldn't be up here."

"Unless you can suggest where he could be, Mr. Crane, I must continue this search in my own way."

"Oh, that's all right, no offence; but we're wasting good time, it seems to me."

"And how would you propose putting in the time to better advantage?"

As Crane had nothing to offer by way of improvement on the detective's methods, the tour of the attics continued.

In rotation, the other stories were searched with the same infinite care. The detective was looking not only for the missing man, but for any clue or indication that might point toward his whereabouts.

Leila grew a little weary of the delay occasioned by such excessive minutiae of searching, but she would not listen to Gale's suggestion that they return to the library and join the others, for she was determined to follow the detective.

Of course a careful investigation was made in Arnold's own rooms, but these were as unproductive as the rest of the house. The rooms on the ground floor also yielded no clue, and, after a search of the kitchens and servants' quarters, Mr. Wheeler started for the cellars.

Both Gale and Leila were interested in the appointments of the basement, for many of its various rooms were fitted up with modern household inventions and domestic appliances. Mr. Crane kept up a running fire of comment on what he saw, and also gave choice bits of unsolicited advice to the detective, whose mind was intent only on letting no obscure bit of space elude his vigilance.

They came at last to the cellars under the oldest part of the house. These, being built in the time of Justin's grandfather, and not having been improved upon since, were quaint and interesting. They were unused, and contained many kitchen utensils and pieces of antique furniture that would have delighted the heart of a collector. But while Gale and Leila paused to examine an old fireplace with a hinged crane, or an old settle or churn, Mr. Wheeler darted from one small room to another, flashing his electric torch everywhere.

"What a lot of old rubbish," exclaimed Crane, who had followed the search through the whole house, futile though he considered it.

"It isn't exactly rubbish," said Leila, who liked antiques. "See this old pewter lamp; this was used for what they called 'burning fluid.' I think these things are interesting. And here's an old workbench, with a,—what is this thing?—attached to it."

"That's a vise," replied Crane. "I suppose someone of Justin's old ancestors used to amuse himself with carpentering now and then. But we're not finding out anything. I believe I'll go back upstairs. I daresay Mabel is looking for me."

But just as Crane turned toward the stairs, Detective Wheeler suddenly appeared in the doorway of the room they were in.

"Miss Duane," he said peremptorily, and in a quick, excited voice, "go upstairs at once."

"Why?" demanded Leila, in surprise, but a glance at Wheeler's face impelled her to obey him.

"Don't ask why," he went on gravely. "Go back upstairs at once—and join the others in the library, or wherever they are, and stay there. Mr. Gale, please remain here."

Leila was already on the staircase, an old flight of wooden steps, and Gale was about to follow her, when detained by Wheeler.

Realizing that ill news was impending, Gale waited only until Leila had disappeared through the door at the head of the stairs, and had closed it behind her, then, turning to Wheeler, he said, "Where is he?"

"Come," returned the detective, and led the way to the next room, where the two footmen stood shivering and with horror-stricken faces. It was a small apartment, with walls that had once been whitewashed, but were now blackened with age. It contained one or two old tables and broken chairs, and a large brick structure with an iron door. Although Gale had only indefinite knowledge of such a thing, he knew at once it was the door of an old-fashioned brick oven.

The oven was an enormous affair, built against the cellar wall, and in shape not unlike a great safe. It was, of course, connected with the chimney, and had doubtless baked the bread of the original Arnolds who built the house. There was a big iron door to it, and a smaller one below, where the fuel was put in.

"We have solved the mystery," said Mr. Wheeler, very gravely, "and it is a tragedy. Be prepared for the worst."

He opened the door of the huge old bake-oven, and within Emory Gale saw the bent body of a man, fully dressed.

"It is Justin!" he exclaimed. "It is murder! It cannot be suicide, can it?"

"Not unless the man was really demented," said Wheeler. "I think, Mr. Gale, we should send for the coroner at once, but I think it wiser to take out the body and examine it first."

"But is it not forbidden to touch a body until the coroner arrives?"

"That is a fallacy believed in by many people, but untrue. I think, if you agree, Mr. Gale, our wisest course is to learn any further detail we may concerning Mr. Arnold's death—for he is certainly dead—before we make a report upstairs." In the excitement of the moment, both men had forgotten Fred Crane, who stood in the background, as dumb with horror as were the two servants. It was somewhat to Crane's credit that he offered no advice at this juncture, but stepped forward and announced himself entirely at Mr. Wheeler's orders, if he could be of any assistance.

The two footmen were practically useless, and it devolved on the others to remove the body of Justin Arnold from the old oven and lay it upon a table. "Good heavens!" exclaimed Gale, with a little gasp, "there's the sofa-pillow!"

The green silk sofa-pillow which had been missed by Leila lay against Arnold's breast, and was bound about his body by its own gilt cord, which had been torn from its edges.

With his usual swift, deft movements, Mr. Wheeler unbound the pillow, and, turning to the others, said, "You see! Mr. Arnold was stabbed through the heart, probably while in the library, for the murderer has bound this pillow over the wound to staunch the flow of blood."

There was no doubt about it, and the detective's statement of facts made the others realize that this was no time for emotion or grief, but a stern situation to be met and coped with. Suppressing a sob, Emory Gale said, "You are quite right, Mr. Wheeler; there is no doubt poor old Justin has been murdered. It only remains for us now to do all we can to break it gently to the others, and to attend to the sad details for them. I thank you, Mr. Wheeler, for your thoughtful tact in sending Miss Duane away before you disclosed the tragedy."

"Yes, yes," returned Wheeler, his mind preoccupied with various details of what his own duties now must be.

As the detective had now performed his task, and the case must go to the coroner and the police, Emory Gale accepted, at least temporarily, the directorship of the situation.

"You two men," he said to the shuddering footmen, "must stay here in reverent charge of your master's body, until some official shall come to relieve you. Mr. Wheeler, you must do whatever your judgment dictates, and Mr. Crane and I will take upon ourselves the task of informing the family."

"Yes, yes, quite right," said Wheeler; "quite a correct arrangement. I will go upstairs with you, as of course you must know, gentlemen, that after more immediate details are attended to we must find the wretch who murdered Mr. Arnold."

"Who could it have been?" exclaimed Fred Crane, realizing for the first time that they were in the presence of an even greater tragedy than that of death.

"That's not a question to be asked now, and perhaps not to be answered soon," replied Wheeler. "Come, let us go upstairs."

The three men went to the library, where all of the others were assembled. Leila's sudden and frightened appearance among them had led them to expect some startling development, but they were all unprepared for the news they must hear. Though a terrible ordeal, Emory Gale was obliged to tell the story, but the .audience had already read in the faces of the three men more than a hint of a tragedy.

"What has become of Justin Arnold is no longer a mystery," Gale began, and though he knew his deepest sympathies should be for Dorothy and Miss Wadsworth, yet his glance wandered uncontrollably to Leila. "We know what has happened to him; and it is the most tragic fate that could overtake a man." He hesitated a moment, and then, realizing that perhaps it were kinder to end the suspense, he added in a low tone, "He has been killed."

To the credit of the nerves of the women present, not one of them fainted or made any outcry. Dorothy put her head down on her mother's shoulder and wept softly. Leila and Mabel Crane were stunned by the news, but bore it with outward calm.

Miss Wadsworth, with a manner highly indicative of her own strength of character, sat bolt upright in her chair and looked steadily at Gale. "I don't quite understand," she said, and the tremble in her voice was pathetic. "What do you mean, Mr. Gale?"

"I cannot bear to tell you the details, Miss Wadsworth," said Gale, with a pitying glance at the old lady; "but the simple and dreadful fact is that we have discovered Justin's body, and have learned that he was murdered—by whom we do not know."

Miss Wadsworth almost fainted, as she at last realized what had happened.

Ernest Chapin rose and went to her side, but as he sat down by her he found himself unable to speak. Campbell Crosby, too, though he essayed to say something, found his voice choked beyond utterance.

CHAPTER 15: THE SCARLET SAGE

LEILA DUANE spoke first. "Who did it?" she asked in a small, shocked voice.

"We don't know yet," replied Mr. Wheeler. "It is a mystery. But the murderer must be found and brought to justice. Had Mr. Arnold any enemies?"

"No," said Campbell Crosby; "and if he had, they couldn't get into this house in the night. Do you know, Mr. Wheeler, how it is locked and barred?"

"Yes. I've heard about it and tried the alarm, and all that. But, Mr. Crosby, we must conclude somebody did force an entrance. Unless we allow ourselves to suspect some member of the household or one of the servants of this dreadful deed."

"Oh, no!" cried Mabel Crane. "That is unthinkable! Someone must have gained entrance from outside, in some way or other."

Mr. Wheeler looked deeply thoughtful. "Although," he went on, "the work for which I was employed is accomplished, I will, if I may, continue to direct affairs here for a brief period. It is necessary that the coroner be summoned at once, and as upon his arrival he will take full charge of the case, I assume I may consider my services no longer required."

But Miss Wadsworth was of a sort that could rise to an emergency. Bravely striving to put aside her grief, she forced herself to consider the immediate requirements of the case.

"Mr. Wheeler," she began, "you have indeed accomplished the work for which you were employed, but, for my part, I do not feel ready to dispense with your services. We have found my cousin"—here the old voice trembled, but immediately became steady again— "now

we must find his murderer and avenge his death. An
Arnold shall not be killed without every effort being to
bring justice to the miserable wretch who committed the
deed! In so far as I have any authority, I wish to employ
you, Mr. Wheeler, to discover whose was the hand that
killed him."

Mr. Wheeler merely bowed in acknowledgment of
this, for he was not quite sure that Miss Wadsworth was
sufficiently in authority to employ him.

"Although I have been seemingly directing matters
here," said Emory Gale, "it is not now my province to
continue. My partner, Mr. Crosby, is Justin Arnold's
cousin, and is naturally heir to his estate, unless it be
otherwise willed. Campbell Crosby therefore ought now to
assume his place as head of this house."

Crosby's handsome face looked disturbed and
troubled. It seemed as if he were unwilling to profit thus
suddenly by his cousin's terrible death. Indeed, all
present were unnerved and bewildered by the shock they
had received, and it was difficult for any of them to think
coherently.

When Campbell Crosby spoke, it was not directly in
reply to Gale's suggestion.

"It seems to me," he said slowly, almost as if thinking
aloud, "that, even before notifying the coroner, we should
send for Justin's family physician."

"Of course," agreed Mr. Wheeler, in his quick way; "I
should have thought of that myself. But I'm
unaccustomed to managing outside my own field of labor,
and I confess I did not think of it. Certainly we must send
for the doctor."

The men began to pull themselves together, and if
Mr. Crane was perhaps a little over-officious in his offers
of assistance, those more nearly related to the dead man
were glad to have his aid.

So Mr. Crane telephoned for Doctor Gaspard, and
took it upon himself to go and notify the servants of the

tragedy, incidentally taking the opportunity to give them some orders on his own account.

Mr. Crane rarely had opportunity to give orders to a corps of trained servants, and he thought it no harm to snatch his chance when it offered. Meantime, Mr. Wheeler notified the coroner, and advised him to come as soon as possible.

"It is perfectly clear," said Wheeler to Campbell Crosby, whom he now looked upon as the head of the house, "that the murderer must have been someone already in the house, as of course no one could get in after the alarm was turned on. Therefore, Mr. Crosby, I'm sure you will agree with me in thinking it was either one of the servants or some intruder who was concealed in the house during the evening."

"I think your second theory is better," said Crosby thoughtfully. "I cannot believe it of one of the servants. They are nearly all old and trustworthy retainers. And he was such a kind master— who could have had a motive?"

"I know so little about Mr. Arnold, I cannot yet judge," said the detective, "but surely, with this sealed house, it cannot be difficult to discover which of its inmates is guilty."

"It would seem so," agreed Crosby; "and yet sometimes what seem to be the simplest cases turn out the most complex."

The two indulged in no further theorizing just then, for Doctor Gaspard arrived. He immediately went downstairs to see what he could learn from an examination of the body of Justin Arnold. On his return he had little to report further than they already knew.

He said that Arnold had been killed by a stab from some long, pointed instrument, probably a dagger. The deed must have been done so swiftly that the victim could not even cry out. The fact of the body being placed where the flue of the chimney made a continuous draft had caused it to remain in a state of preservation. The sofa-pillow had been placed immediately against Arnold's breast in order that no blood might fall from the wound. It had then doubtless been bound to the body, by its own cord, hastily torn off, and the body carried to the cellar.

The fact that the pillow had been used seemed to show that the murder had been committed in the library, and the body taken downstairs for the purpose of concealment. How the murderer came or went, of course the doctor could not even suggest. That was a matter to be taken up later by the detective.

Aside from his professional interest in the Arnold family, Doctor Gaspard had always been a warm friend, both of Justin and his father. The present tragedy almost unnerved the old gentleman, and, though he remained to luncheon, he ate scarcely anything, and seemed unable to shake off his depression.

Nor did the others have any appetite for the meal. The dreadful happening seemed to have changed everything, and made even the ordinary routine of the day seem strange and distorted. Dorothy's pretty face looked white and drawn, and her dark eyes seemed twice their normal size. Leila, less personally interested, was excited by the strangeness and mystery of it all. She wanted to set to work at once to discover the criminal, and waited impatiently for the coroner and his hoped-for revelations.

The luncheon over, various groups gathered here and there to talk about the subject that engrossed them all.

Just before he left the house, Doctor Gaspard looked about him in a sort of bewildered way. He looked at Miss Wadsworth, and then shook his head. He glanced at the detective, Mr. Wheeler, and started toward him as he stood on the verandah, but just before the doctor reached him, the detective turned hurriedly to speak to someone else.

"What is it, Doctor Gaspard," said Fred Crane; "can I do anything for you?"

"It's only this." The doctor spoke undecidedly, and in low tones.

"Let us step down the path," said Crane, leading the other down the steps and along the garden walk.

"Now tell me."

"It's probably nothing of any account. But I want to tell somebody about it. I tried to get hold of the detective."

"Tell me, doctor. I am helping Mr. Wheeler, and doubtless I can repeat your message to him better than the others."

"Very well, Mr. Crane. It is this. When I made the examination of poor Justin's body, and found the stab wound, I found nothing else indicative or unusual, except this." Dr. Gaspard took from a pocketbook a small sprig of scarlet sage. It was withered and crushed, but intact. "This was tightly clasped in Justin's dead hand. I was about to throw it away, when I thought it might be of value as evidence in hunting the criminal. I know nothing of detective work, and 'clues' as they call them, but I felt I must save this. Was it foolish?"

"Not at all," said Fred Crane, more to humor the old man than because he thought the "clue" of any consequence. "If you will entrust it to me, Doctor, I will see that Mr. Wheeler gets it, and I will tell him where you found it."

"Thank you, Mr. Crane. Is Wheeler a smart man? Will he find Justin's murderer, do you think?"

"I hope so, I'm sure. It's all so sudden, and such a shock, that we none of us know which way to turn. But of course the murderer must be found, and made to expiate his crime. I'm a sort of detective, myself, and if Wheeler can't lay his finger on the criminal, I shall take the case in hand. I've not interfered in his work, for it was not my place. But my wife is a cousin of the Arnold family, and I shan't fed that I'm doing my duty unless I help all I can to avenge this crime."

Doctor Gaspard went away, and Crane put the withered blossom in his own pocketbook, smiling a little at the deed. "It's of no earthly use," he thought. "To find the weapon the man was killed with is the thing to do.

I'm going to start in by looking for that. If I find it, I rather guess old Wheeler will open his eyes."

Crane made at once for the cellar. The body of Justin Arnold was lying on a table, covered with a sheet and guarded by the two white-faced footmen. They stood immovable as sentries, and after a word with them, Crane began his search. He hunted everywhere for a dirk or dagger, looking behind benches and into cupboards and dark alcoves where it might have been thrown.

CHAPTER 16: THE CORONER'S QUESTIONS

ERNEST CHAPIN found himself alone with Dorothy for a moment, on the Terrace.

"I can't talk about it!" he exclaimed, as if in agony. "How can those other men discuss it as if it were an every-day business affair? They propose coroners and detectives as if they were ordering workmen about."

"I feel as you do, Ernest," said Dorothy. "All this discussion drives me frantic. I can't bring myself even to think about it calmly. And Leila is crazy to do 'detective work,' as she calls it, and find out who—who—"

"Don't try to say it, dear; and don't judge Leila too harshly. You know she was not so close to Justin as you were."

For the moment, Chapin seemed to ignore his own love for Dorothy in his rush of emotion for poor Arnold, but the next instant a realization came to him of what Arnold's death really meant to her, and he took a step toward her, whispering exultantly, "But you are now freed from him, and you are mine!"

"Oh, Ernest, don't!" cried Dorothy, in accents almost of agony, and then, leaving him abruptly, she almost ran back into the house.

Chapin stood leaning against a pillar, gazing out into vacancy across the gardens, when a swift motorcar whizzed up the drive and two strange men got out.

Instinctively, Chapin knew it was the coroner and his assistant and he greeted them with forced courtesy.

"Coroner Fiske, I suppose?" he said, and, being answered in the affirmative, he showed the men into the house, where they were met by Crosby and Gale.

If Detective Wheeler's methods were systematic and expeditious, Coroner Fiske's were even more so. Though told at once that Mr. Crosby was now head of the house, he singled out Mr. Crane to answer his questions and to act as his guide. This he did because Crane was neither a relative nor so close a friend of the dead man as the others. Accompanied by the aide he had brought, and led by Crane, he went at once to the cellar. The official examination only corroborated what the doctor had already said.

"Where is the weapon?" asked the coroner.but as nobody had seen it, or even thought about it, he received no answer.

"That is enough," he said at last, and then gave directions that the body of the late Justin Arnold be removed to a more fitting place.

Then Mr. Fiske went back rapidly to the library, and announced to Campbell Crosby and Miss Wadsworth that he would hold a preliminary investigation then and there.

"It isn't exactly an inquest," he explained, "but it will be a searching investigation, and I must have every member of the household—family, guests, and servants—present or within immediate call."

In an incredibly short time all save a few of the servants had assembled in the library, and the investigation was begun.

"As the circumstances are unusual," said Mr. Fiske, "and, as far as we can see for the moment, the deed was probably committed by someone already within the walls, I must ask every one of you to answer readily and promptly any and all questions, without feeling in any case that query means suspicion. It is necessary that every one should tell everything he knows of the events of the night on which the murder was committed; for an incident of seemingly slight importance sometimes proves to be the very key to the mystery. Mr. Crosby, as present head of the house, I will question you first. At what hour did you last see Mr. Arnold on Monday night?"

Campbell Crosby started in amazement, and then realized that the coroner was not in possession of all the circumstances.

"I was not here Monday night," he said. "I had been here spending the week-end, but Mr. Gale and myself returned to Philadelphia on the afternoon train. From there we were summoned here yesterday by the tidings of my cousin's death."

"You were, then, in Philadelphia Monday evening. What were you doing?"

Crosby looked as if inclined to resent this absurd questioning of one who was not present at the time of the crime, but the thought flashed across him that, as he was his cousin's legal heir, perhaps he would be subjected to close questioning.

"I dined at my hotel," he replied, "and afterward went to a concert."

"And after that?"

"It was fairly late when the concert was over, and I went back to the hotel and turned in."

But though Crosby stood this questioning without comment, Gale was not willing to do so.

"If you'll excuse me, Mr. Coroner," he said, "you are wasting your time in asking questions concerning this matter of my partner or myself. Mr. Crosby telephoned me three or four times during the evening, and as we met at our law office Tuesday morning, and proceeded to our work for the day, I think we need not be further cross-questioned in connection with this matter."

"That is true, that is true," said Mr. Fiske, and he nervously tapped his pencil on the table before him, while Leila with her quick-witted intelligence immediately surmised that he was asking these questions by way of killing time, because he dreaded getting to the real truth of the matter. Leila had her own suspicions, and they were growing stronger every minute, until to her they seemed almost a certainty, and she wondered if every one else suspected the same culprit.

Coroner Fiske sighed, readjusted his spectacles, and turned next to Miss Wadsworth.

"You are housekeeper here?" he inquired courteously.

"Not housekeeper exactly," said Miss Abby, tossing her head ever so slightly. "Mrs. Garson has that position. I am Justin Arnold's cousin, or, rather, his father's cousin. This has always been my home, and my position is that of lady of the house."

"And will you please tell me the time and occasion of your last interview with Mr. Arnold?"

"There was no especial interview," said Miss Abby, a little crisply, for she had taken a dislike to the coroner. "After dinner Monday evening we all sat in the drawing-room. Then the ladies of the party, including myself, all went to their rooms at about twelve o'clock, I should think. I fancy the men did not stay down much later, for I heard them coming up about half-past twelve. Further than that, I can tell you nothing of the events of Monday night."

Mrs. Duncan and Mrs. Crane were questioned next, but what they said was merely a repetition of Miss Wadsworth's testimony.

Then the coroner's attention was turned to Dorothy. The girl was desperately frightened, for Chapin had made her promise not to tell of their meeting on the balcony, and if she kept this promise, she could not be entirely truthful in her testimony. So, in response to Mr. Fiske's inquiry, she asserted that she had gone upstairs with the other ladies at twelve o'clock, and that she had stopped for a short time in Miss Duane's room and had chatted there for perhaps twenty minutes, when she went to her own room.

"You heard nothing of the gentlemen belowstairs?" asked the coroner.

"I may have heard their voices from the hall," said Dorothy carelessly; "but I paid no attention to them, and went directly to my own room."

Leila Duane looked at Dorothy with such a meaning glance that Dorothy realized at once that Leila knew she was telling an untruth. As a matter of fact, Leila had heard Dorothy and Chapin conversing in low tones, and had even heard their steps as they went out to the balcony.

But Leila said nothing either then or when, a few moments later, she herself was called upon to answer questions. She simply repeated Dorothy's story, and corroborated the statement that Dorothy left her (Leila's) room at fifteen or twenty minutes past twelve.

Satisfied that the women could tell him nothing of importance, the coroner turned to the men. Mr. Gale and Mr. Crosby having already been questioned, Mr. Chapin was next interviewed. As confidential secretary, he answered various questions about Justin Arnold's financial affairs and personal habits. Being asked concerning his last interview with Mr. Arnold, he merely said that after the ladies had left them on Monday night, the men went for a short time to the smoking-room. He said that he and Mr. Crane bade Justin Arnold goodnight at about half-past twelve, and went at once to their own rooms. He stated that they left Mr. Arnold in the smoking-room, as it was his habit always to stay up after his guests retired.

"And you never saw Mr. Arnold alive again, after leaving him at that time?" inquired the coroner.

"No," replied Chapin, but his voice was low, and he shot a furtive glance at Dorothy, who dropped her own eyes before it.

However, there was no reason to doubt Mr. Chapin's statements, and Mr. Crane, who was called next, corroborated them so far as his own movements were concerned. He deposed that he had said good-night to his host at half-past twelve, and went away with Chapin. Their ways diverged, however, as they were quartered far apart in the big house. Mr. Crane had gone directly to his own room, and had heard nothing strange or unusual through the night.

"Then," said the coroner, by way of summing up, "I am informed that none of the family or guests saw Mr. Arnold after half-past twelve on Monday night. I will, therefore, now put some inquiries to the servants."

"Excuse me," said Emory Gale. "I have no wish to seem intrusive or to put any unnecessary query; but as the late Mr. Arnold's lawyer I claim a right to assist in the investigation of this case. I have waited for Mr. Arnold's secretary to make a statement which he has not made, but which I cannot think he has any objection to making. Mr. Chapin has previously informed me that Mr. Arnold drew a check to his, Chapin's, order for a large amount of money. As this check was drawn after midnight on Monday, it was dated Tuesday. As I was in Philadelphia that night, I know little of the matter; but I wish to inquire if this check was drawn while the gentlemen were in the smoking-room with Mr. Arnold between twelve and twelve-thirty."

"It was not," quickly volunteered Fred Crane, who never could refrain from giving information. "I was there all that time, and we were telling stories and chatting, and no business matter of any kind was brought up."

There was a dead silence, for everybody saw the implication. If Chapin had received that check after twelve o'clock, and if it had not been drawn while the men were in the smoking-room, then Chapin must have returned for a further interview with Justin Arnold after leaving Crane at twelve-thirty!

"Will you explain this apparent discrepancy in your statements, Mr. Chapin?" asked the coroner coldly, but courteously enough.

"The explanation is," said Chapin sullenly, "that I did go back to speak to Arnold for a moment, and he gave me the check. As it is private business of my own, I cannot see that I need answer further questions concerning it."

"Not concerning the business, Mr. Chapin," said the coroner; "but this would seem to indicate that you are the last person known to have seen Mr. Arnold alive."

Ernest Chapin's entire manner changed. His sullenness turned to wrath. His eyes flashed, and a red spot burned in either cheek as he almost shouted, "What do you mean by such an implication? Suppose I did see Mr. Arnold again that night! I know nothing of his death or of his murderer!"

"It would be wiser, Mr. Chapin," said Mr. Fiske coldly, "to show less excitement over the statement of your innocence."

"Perhaps it would be wiser, but it is not easy to be wise, under such unjust implications."

"Then if they are so unjust, why not tell us frankly why Mr. Arnold gave you that large check."

"Because you have no right to ask, and I do not choose to tell. It has no bearing on the question of Mr. Arnold's death, and I fail to see why I should enlighten you regarding my private business affairs."

"But you quarrelled with Mr. Arnold."

"I do not admit that. But if we had a few high words, again you must be satisfied to learn that the purport of them was entirely foreign to the cause of this inquiry you are conducting."

Chapin's manner was not rude, but it was curt and gave no invitation for further questioning. The coroner looked at him sternly for a moment and then dismissed him as a witness. But it was plain to be seen Mr. Fiske was by no means through with him, and would doubtless question him further at the formal inquest next day.

There was a brief and not very pleasant silence. Everybody felt uncomfortable at Chapin's attitude, and also at the coroner's hints.

While not a general favorite, Ernest Chapin was known and liked by all present, and the idea of his being concerned in the crime was too unthinkable. Fred Crane at last created a divertisement. "Oh, I forgot something," he said, suddenly; "it may be a clue. Doctor Gaspard gave me this, Mr. Fiske. He found it tightly clasped in Mr. Arnold's hand."

As he spoke, Crane gave the coroner the withered sprig of scarlet sage.

"Why was that not given to me?" inquired Detective Wheeler, abruptly.

"I forgot all about it," confessed Crane; "I can't see now that it means anything."

"Of course it means something," said Wheeler; "it doubtless means that the murderer of Mr. Arnold was wearing that flower in his buttonhole, and the dying man clutched at it."

"Drawing a pretty long bow," said Campbell Crosby, doubtfully; "of course that might be true, but so might lots of other conclusions, I think."

"For instance?" inquired Wheeler, a little ironically. "Why, lots of that flower is all about the house; Justin might easily have had a bit in his hand, or, for that matter, it might have been in his own buttonhole. He often wore it."

Mabel Crane looked up with startled eyes. She glanced at Leila Duane, wondering if she remembered her story of seeing Dorothy go downstairs late Monday night. Dorothy had worn a white gown and a bunch of scarlet sage at her belt. Certainly Dorothy had been downstairs after the hour at which Ernest Chapin said he went up, but with that little flirt, there was no telling what she might have done. And yet, Mabel couldn't bring herself to raise the question. She looked at Dorothy, she even looked at her inquiringly, but the girl in no way responded to her glances.

In fact, Dorothy sat like one turned to stone. Her great, dark eyes were fixed on the coroner's face, and her whole form was rigid and immovable. But her hands were clenched as if she were at the end of her nervous strength.

Mr. Wheeler took the scarlet blossom and put it away in his pocketbook, remarking that it might yet prove useful.

Then Mabel Crane, unable longer to keep silent, spoke out.

"As it can't possibly do any harm," she said, "I will tell of something I saw. I saw Miss Duncan come downstairs at nearly two o'clock on Monday night,—"

"I did not!" interrupted Dorothy; "you are mistaken."

"But I saw you, and you were wearing a bunch of that flower."

"Why, Mabel Crane! What do you mean! Are you saying I killed Justin?" Dorothy looked like an avenging angel, and sat up straight, with a look of horror and indignation on her beautiful face.

"No!" cried Mabel, in amazement, "certainly not! I only meant you might have given Justin the flower, before the burglar, or whoever killed him, came in."

"But I didn't come down at two o'clock," insisted Dorothy. "I was in bed and asleep at that hour."

"But I saw you!" and Mabel looked puzzled.

"Why should you deny it? Did you see Mr. Chapin down here?"

"No, I did not! Because I didn't come down, I tell you! I went upstairs with the rest of you, and I was in Leila's room for a while and then I went to bed."

Coroner Fiske looked from one to the other of the speakers. Both were so positive in their assertions, it was hard to tell which was telling the truth. And yet one must be telling a falsehood. What motive could Mrs. Crane have for doing so? And, if Dorothy did come down she must know more than she had yet told. To connect her with the crime was not possible, but she might have given the flower, and she might have seen something that she wouldn't tell. Could she have seen Chapin, or some intruder? Certainly she was concealing something.

But Mabel Crane was not satisfied to let the matter drop.

"Why, I told Leila Duane that I saw you! Didn't I, Leila?"

"Yes," returned Leila, unwillingly.

"You're mistaken," said Dorothy again, and the coroner asked nothing further then.

CHAPTER 17: THE WEAPON

FUNERAL services for Justin Arnold were to be held the next morning, and the formal inquest would be begun Thursday afternoon.

Because of the painful circumstances, there would not be elaborate obsequies, and the mourners at the funeral would comprise only the household and a few personal friends and neighbors. Wednesday evening was a trying time for everybody. The women were on the verge of nervous breakdown, and the men were taciturn and gloomy.

The matter of Justin Arnold's will was discussed, and though the instrument itself was in the safe of Gale & Crosby's office, the lawyers knew its contents, and these they made known to the rest.

"The will provides," said Emory Gale, "a legacy of one hundred thousand dollars to Miss Wadsworth; fifty thousand dollars to Ernest Chapin; and good-sized bequests to all of the servants, the largest, of course, for those who have been longest in Mr. Arnold's employ."

"I am positive," spoke up Fred Crane, "that the murderer is one of the servants. In fact, it must be. Someone of them knew of the legacy coming to him, and killed his master in order to obtain his money at once."

"I'm sure that is so," said Dorothy eagerly, for she realized only too well that dark thoughts had been directed toward Ernest Chapin, and she welcomed a suggestion that the criminal might be one of the servants.

"To proceed with the terms of the will," went on Emory Gale, "after some further bequests to a few relatives, friends, and charities, the entire residuary estate, including White Birches, is left to Campbell Crosby."

"Of course this is not a surprise to me," said Crosby, speaking gravely, as one who had just incurred a great responsibility, "for Justin made this will years ago, and as one of his lawyers I of course knew of it Moreover, as his next of kin, it was quite right that I should inherit the property, at the time the will was made. But since then Justin became engaged to Miss Duncan, and upon their marriage she would have become his heir. Moreover, Justin told me only a short time ago that he proposed making a new will, which should leave all his property to his wife, irrespective of her legal rights thereto. I thought it probable that my cousin had made a personal will or perhaps a memorandum to that effect, which, if it were found, I should consider as binding as a legally attested instrument. So far nothing of the sort has been found, but it may yet come to light As the one chiefly interested, I should like to suggest that we leave the matter of inheritance unconsidered for the present, paying from the estate such minor legacies as may be deemed advisable."

This speech of Crosby's had a good effect upon them all. It seemed to dispel a little the vague gloom of the atmosphere, and put matters upon a more practical basis. As a matter of fact, though all felt the horror of the crime, no one present felt a poignant sorrow at Arnold's death. He had not been a lovable man, and though Miss Wadsworth had lived peaceably with him, they had few interests in common, and their relations were in no way affectionate. As for Dorothy, she seemed to have awakened. She knew now she had never loved Arnold, that she had promised to marry him only because she was dazzled by his wealth and position. And now Campbell Crosby was his heir, and Campbell Crosby was desperately in love with her, but fickle little Dorothy knew her own heart at last, and knew that she had given it irrevocably into Ernest Chapin's keeping. The facts that Chapin was acting queerly, that he had not adhered strictly to truth in his statements, and that men who had known him for years were already thinking horrible thoughts about him,—all these things had no weight with Dorothy. She knew that he had suppressed the story of the scene on the balcony to shield her own good name. She knew that he had returned downstairs with Arnold. What had then happened she would not dare to think, but she would have no suspicion in her own mind of the man she loved. And so, absorbed in her realization of these things, Dorothy did not sincerely mourn Justin Arnold, though shocked and horrified by the tragedy of his death.

However, if the men felt in anyway uncertain of Chapin's integrity, they did not show it by actual word or deed. Perhaps their manner was a trifle constrained, and they did not ask his opinion or defer to his judgment as much as they might have done. Crosby, however, was an exception to this. He rather went out of his way to be pleasant to Chapin, and seemed to indicate, that for his part he had no ill thought of the man.

"I think," he said, speaking to the company in general, "that since the inquest will be formally conducted to-morrow afternoon, it is advisable for us to decide upon some uniform course of action. That coroner will endeavor to make us express opinions in support of his own theories, whether we entirely believe them or not. Mr. Fiske is shrewd, and rather clever at suggesting answers to his own questions. Now, personally, I do not for a moment believe that Justin was killed by any of his servants, nor anyone else who was staying in the house that night. I believe that some intruder or burglar effected an entrance and killed my cousin. Don't ask me how he got in,—we have discussed that question from all points. But I hold that some such outsider did get in and did commit the crime. Now, if any of you can conscientiously agree with me, I hope you will so frame your answers to the coroner's questions that they will support that theory."

The others looked at him with varying expressions, as if considering this mode of procedure. "I know you're right!" exclaimed Dorothy; "and I for one shall tell Mr. Fiske so in plain words!"

"I'm afraid, Dorothy, your plain words will have little effect on the coroner's verdict," said Gale.

He spoke listlessly, as if whatever might be said by a preconcerted decision would have little weight with the stern decision of justice.

Ernest Chapin said nothing in response to Crosby's suggestion, but he moved about restlessly and finally left the room. Soon the rest of the party broke up into smaller groups, and Leila made an opportunity for a few words alone with Dorothy.

"Are you going to tell the truth when you're questioned to-morrow?" Leila said, looking Dorothy straight in the eyes.

"What do you mean?" And Dorothy looked angrily at her friend.

"You know very well what I mean. When you left my room that night you did not go at once to your own room. I heard you speak to Ernest Chapin in the corridor; I heard you go out with him to the little balcony."

"Did you hear anything more?" and Dorothy's eyes grew wide with fear.

"No; I thought it was none of my business."

"That's exactly what I think!"

"But it will be my business if you give false evidence!"

"Gracious, Leila! don't talk like a professional detective! Suppose I did flirt with, Mr. Chapin, it wasn't the first time,—and it won't be the last, either. But I see no reason why I should tell Mr. Fiske about it."

"Tell Mr. Fiske about what?" asked Emory Gale, as he and Crosby joined the girls in the alcove where they were standing.

Before Dorothy could reply, Leila, in her endeavor to prove to Gale her detective, ability, told the whole story.

Dorothy pouted; "I think you're mean, Leila, to tell that; but I really don't suppose it makes any difference. Mr. Gale, do I have to tell the coroner that I saw Mr.

Chapin for a few minutes after he came upstairs that night?"

Though the question was addressed to Gale, Crosby answered it. "Of course you don't, Dorothy," he said; "I suppose Chapin told you not to, didn't he?"

"Yes, but how, did you know that?"

"I only surmised it," said Crosby, smiling down at her startled face; "now, it's perfectly clear that Chapin wants to suppress that bit of information, because there's no earthly use of the fact being known that you were indiscreet enough to meet him so late at night."

"It was only for a minute," pouted Dorothy. "I know it, my dear child; and there's no harm done if you keep quiet about it, which Chapin was quite right to ask you to do. I hope, Miss Duane, you won't consider it your duty to make the story public. Persuade her not to, Gale; Dorothy and I will give you opportunity."

Crosby took Dorothy by the arm and led her out to the South Terrace. He caught up a wrap as they passed through the hall, and deftly flung it round her shoulders, for the evening was chill.

In silence, he led her to the very end of the terrace, and they stood looking at the moon, now slightly on its wane, and partly obscured by passing clouds. He drew the voluminous silken cape more closely round her, and, still holding its fulness at her throat, he tilted her dainty chin until her eyes looked into his own.

"Dorothy," he said, "darling, I can't wait! You must promise me now that you will be mine; that you will marry me, after all these horrible scenes are over. Promise me, darling, and then, if you insist, I will wait patiently for a time. But let me have your dear promise, let me know that there is hope for me—"

"But there isn't any, Campbell;" and Dorothy spoke very seriously, while a troubled look came into her eyes.

"You don't mean that, darling;" and Crosby was very gentle and tender. "You don't mean I mayn't hope, for I couldn't live without that! What you really mean is that you can't think about it now; your dear little heart is so perturbed by these dreadful scenes. I'm a brute even to think you can tell me now what I want to know. But you will, sweetheart, you will! And after a time we will be happy together, Dorothy. White Birches is mine now, and I care, dear, only because I can offer it to you."

Dorothy moved slightly aside from Crosby's nearness. "Campbell," she said, in a faint little voice, "I've a good mind to confide in you."

"Why shouldn't you, dearest? Tell me anything you wish. It will be perfectly safe with me."

"Well, Justin knew that Mr. Chapin and I were on the balcony that night. He found us there together. And he was very angry. He sent me to my room, and asked Mr. Chapin to go downstairs with him."

"Oh!" exclaimed Crosby, in a tone of surprise. "I begin to understand."

"But, Campbell—that didn't—that couldn't have had anything to do with—with what happened to Justin!"

"Dorothy, hush!" and Crosby's voice was tense. "Never breathe such a thing! Now, listen: I don't believe for one minute that Ernest Chapin had anything to do with Justin's death, but I can tell you, dear, that there's going to be a most fearful lot of circumstantial evidence piled up against him. That evidence, Dorothy, you and I will fight!"

"Whether it's true or not?"

"Whether it's true or not."

"Oh, Campbell, even—I hate to say it, but even if Ernest Chapin was—did do wrong, could you get him off? You're a lawyer, you know."

Crosby's face changed. He stepped nearer to Dorothy and grasped her shoulders. "Why do you say that?" he said hoarsely. "Why are you so desperately anxious to have him cleared of suspicion? Dorothy, it can't be that you care for him!"

"That has nothing to do with it," said Dorothy, haughtily.

"It has everything to do with it!" And Campbell clasped her almost roughly in his arms. "Tell me—tell me this instant—do you really care for that ordinary, uninteresting fellow, who is not really of your own class?"

"He isn't ordinary and uninteresting! You shan't say such things!"

"Then, you do care for him! Why, Dorothy, he's beneath you in every way!"

"Love levels all ranks," said the girl softly.

Crosby looked at her a moment, as if in utter despair. Then his face suddenly changed, and he said exultantly, "I'm not afraid! I know you for a fickle young person, and even though you think for the moment that you're interested in that man, it's partly because you think he's a martyr, and more because you never know your own mind two days in succession! But I'm going to teach you, you beautiful little rogue, you, what it means to be true and constant to one love only. My love for you is so big and desperate that I will compel you to love me, and me alone! Do you hear that, my beauty?"

Dorothy was really frightened at Crosby's vehemence, for, though she had received impassioned declarations before, there was something in this man's manner that made her feel his power over her. Under the effect of it, she almost wavered for an instant in her loyalty to Chapin; but Dorothy was beginning to find herself, and her new-born loyalty to the man she really loved was already strong enough to withstand temptation. But she knew instinctively that to declare further her love for Chapin would enrage Crosby, and possibly cause him to withhold whatever influence he might have toward clearing Ernest of any possible suspicion; So she gently forbade Crosby to continue his own pleadings at the present time, and with tender consideration he changed the subject and again became his own debonair, interesting self.

At last they went back into the house, and the sudden hush that fell on the party assembled in the living-room told Dorothy they had been talking about her. She knew they all suspected her of untruth regarding her return downstairs the night of the murder. But Mabel Crane was kind and pleasant as always. She ignored the subject of Dorothy's doings that night and said little about the murder at all.

But her husband was not so reticent. All day he had been hunting the house in an endeavor to find the weapon which had been used, and it chanced to be just as Dorothy entered the room, that he sprang up and grasped the Spanish dagger that lay on the library table. The large room, which was both library and living-room, boasted several library tables and desks, and each was amply furnished with writing paraphernalia. On the others were ordinary paper-knives, of silver or ivory, but on one lay the deadly-looking dagger that Dorothy had played with on the night of the dance the week before.

"There's the weapon!" exclaimed Mr. Crane, and Dorothy turned pale. She remembered how she had pointed it at Justin Arnold in play; and, too, how she had expressed her liking for that sort of thing.

"How do you know it is?" she said with a gasping breath.

Crane looked at her curiously. Surely she was showing great excitement over the matter.

"I don't know for certain, but it was here in this room that the murder was doubtless committed.

That is shown, in all probability, by the use of the sofa-pillow. Well, if this dagger was right here handy, why not suppose the murderer used it?"

"Let me see it," and Wheeler held out his hand for the knife.

"I see some stains near the handle," he said, slowly; "the blade was wiped clean, but there is something in the joint that looks like blood." He took the dagger away with him for a careful test and returned shortly, saying:" Yes, as I thought, that dagger is stained with blood."

"It was cleaned on the sofa-pillow," said Crane;"I noticed the marks. There is no doubt that the murderer used that paper cutter for his awful deed. I'll put it away and show it to Fiske to-morrow."

"But it doesn't prove anything," said Dorothy, almost in a whisper.

All eyes were upon her. She was evidently under a great nervous strain, and her eyes blazed and red spots burned in her cheeks, Emory Gale shuddered as he remembered the words she had used when she playfully threatened Arnold with the dagger. She had said if he ever scolded her she would kill him! Had she come down late at night, as Mrs. Crane insisted, and had Arnold scolded her, and had, Nonsense! he well knew Dorothy was capable of no such deed. But she had said she loved a dagger; that her ancestors must have been pirates and Spanish dancing girls! It was nonsense, of course, for Mrs. Duncan was a most mild-mannered lady, but he had no idea what her father had been like. Perhaps he had been of a murderous disposition,—pshaw! what foolishness was he thinking! He glanced at Crosby. He, too, had heard Dorothy's foolish talk that night, but fortunately, he said to himself, no one else had,—that is, except poor old Arnold. Crosby was watching Dorothy intently. Gale knew he must be thinking of the girl in connection with the dagger. But Gale was wrong in thinking no one else had heard that talk. For Fred Crane that night had chanced to be standing just outside the portiere and had been interested in Dorothy's gay banter.

A little later, Crane asked Dorothy to go with him for a stroll on the verandah. Looking a little surprised and a little frightened, she consented.

"Miss Duncan," Crane began, without preamble, "I am looking up the truths in this case, and I hope to learn the identity of the murderer. Now I'm sure if you know of anything that would help my investigations you will not refuse to tell me. You are worried and nervous, and I don't wonder you don't like to be questioned before the others. But if you will just tell me what you know, I will promise you to be most discreet in using that knowledge."

"I don't understand this request, Mr. Crane," and Dorothy flashed a glance at him. "Perhaps if you will tell me of what you suspect me, I will tell you whether I know anything at all of the matter or not."

"Suspect is too strong a word. I suspect you of nothing worse than withholding knowledge."

"Oh, then you don't think I used that dagger last Monday night?"

"I shouldn't like to think so,—and yet," and Crane looked straight at her; "I will tell you that I chanced to overhear you tell Arnold that you would kill him if he scolded you! Also, that you loved to play with a dagger! A strange admission from a young lady!"

"Eavesdropper!"

"Not at all. I merely happened to be on the other side of the curtain, and hearing such extraordinary statements I was naturally interested. Then, my wife said she saw you come downstairs late that night. Then, Mr. Arnold was found clasping a sprig of scarlet sage, and according to my wife, you were wearing a large bunch, of that flower when you came downstairs."

"And so you think me guilty of murder?"

"I do not. I repeat I do not. But I think you know something that ought to be told in the interests of right and justice."

"And I suppose I don't care to confide to you, if I do have any such knowledge."

"Then you will be obliged to tell it at the inquest. And if you tell me now, it will be much easier for you on that more public occasion."

"Good-night, Mr. Crane," said Dorothy in an icy voice. And then, turning from him she walked away with great dignity. Crane looked after her astounded. He had thought to intimidate her at least, but she went away like a tragedy queen. Her enforced calm did not last long. She went straight to her own room and throwing herself on the bed, gave way to a stormy crying fit. Her mother came tapping at the locked door, but Dorothy told her to go away, saying she had a headache and would see nobody. Her mother coaxed for a time, but in vain, and then went away, leaving poor Dorothy to herself.

CHAPTER 18: THE INQUEST

THE next morning brought the harrowing hours of the funeral, and in the afternoon began the no less disturbing experiences of the coroner's inquest. Mr. Fiske had impanelled a coroner's jury of six men, and the proceedings began directly after luncheon was over.

The coroner had his programme mapped out, and his questions were definite and to the point, bringing out the principal facts in logical order. The informal testimony of the day before was repeated under oath, and soon the jury were in possession of all the evidence given by the members of the household.

Dorothy told her story exactly as she had the day before, excusing it to herself by arguing that she had kept back only part of the truth and had not told an actual falsehood.

Ernest Chapin repeated his story, admitting the receipt of a check of five thousand dollars from Arnold, during an interview which took place after half-past twelve o'clock on Monday night.

But he refused to tell the nature of the interview, or the reason for the check, saying that it was a private matter between him and his employer, and had no bearing upon the crime.

Without comment on Mr. Chapin's statements, Mr. Fiske next questioned the servants.

From Driggs, the butler, the jury learned of Mr. Arnold's peculiar precautions against burglars, of his personal habits, and of his doings, so far as Driggs knew, on the night the crime was committed.

"When did you last see your master alive?" inquired the coroner.

"Just before I went to bed, sir, as I passed through the hall, I saw Mr. Arnold in the library, sir."

"Was he alone?"

"No, sir."

"Who was with him?"

Driggs made so long a pause that the coroner repeated his question. The butler was not apt in the art of deception, for he fidgeted nervously, and cast many furtive glances at Ernest Chapin, then replied, hesitatingly: "I couldn't rightly say, sir. The gentleman's back was toward me."

"Was it a stranger to the house?"

"I—I don't think so, sir."

"You heard his voice?"

"And did you recognize that?"

"Why—yes, sir."

At the end of his endurance, and unable longer to withstand the coroner's insistence, Driggs fairly blurted out, "It was Mr. Chapin, sir."

"As Mr. Chapin has already informed us that he had a late interview with Mr. Arnold, you need not have been so reluctant to say that you saw him," commented the coroner, coldly. "Did the conversation between Mr. Arnold and Mr. Chapin seem to be of a friendly nature?"

"It did not;" Driggs's tone now indicated that he would withhold nothing from his evidence.

"Were they apparently angry?"

"They were, sir."

"Very angry?"

"Very angry, sir."

"Did you overhear any words?"

"I'm not given to eavesdropping, sir."

"Did you overhear any words?" the coroner repeated, and his icy glance seemed to fascinate Driggs.

"I did, then, sir. I heard Mr. Arnold say that many a man had killed another for less than that."

"You heard nothing more?"

"Nothing more at all, sir."

"And then you went directly away to your own quarters?"

"Yes. sir."

"That will do; "and Driggs's testimony was ended.

Although to coroner and jury the butler's evidence had a certain meaning, yet others present seemed disturbed by varying emotions.

Ernest Chapin's face turned scarlet, and he sat with his eyes cast down, the picture of a troubled, despairing man.

Dorothy looked anxiously thoughtful. She knew that Arnold had seen her in Chapin's embrace, and she hadn't the slightest doubt that the words quoted by Driggs referred to that. But surely the quarrel between the two men could not have had such a desperate result as murder, and if it had, the roles of criminal and victim should have been reversed. Both Gale and Crosby seemed deeply interested in Driggs's story. Crosby's glance wandered often to Dorothy, and at times his compressed lips showed his own anger at the thought of the girl he loved being the subject of a quarrel between two other men.

As for Fred Crane, he had simply made up his mind that startling developments were imminent, and he scribbled now and then in a note-book as he sat breathlessly waiting further disclosures. Jane, a chambermaid, was next to be questioned.

"What is your work in this house?" asked the coroner.

"I takes care of some of the bedrooms, sir. Not all of 'em."

"Do you take care of Mr. Arnold's bedroom?"

"Yes, I do that."

"Did you go to make up his room on Tuesday morning?"

"Yes, sir."

"And what did you find?"

"I found the bed just as it was after turnin' it down the night before."

"It had not been slept in, you are sure?"

"I'm sure. It was just exactly as I'd turned it down Monday evenin'. Mr. Arnold is a very particular man, sir; and I always turn his bed most careful. It hadn't been touched since I did so, sir."

"What did you do then?"

"I just made it up smooth again, and put on the day counterpane and roll bolster like I always fixes it for the day, sir."

"Didn't you think it strange that Mr. Arnold had not occupied his room?"

"It's not my business to think, sir. I did my work there and went on."

"And his bath had not been used?"

"No, sir; the towels and sponges were all just as I had left 'em. Not a thing had been touched."

"What did you do next?"

"I—I went next to make up Mr. Chapin's room, sir."

"Well, was there anything unusual there?"

"Unusual, sir?"

"You heard me! What was unusual about Mr. Chapin's room? Hadn't his bed been slept in, either?"

"Yes, oh, yes, sir. It had. I went to work and made it up, sir."

"And then?"

"Then I put the room to rights and dusted it and—and tidied everything."

"Jane, you are keeping something back. What was unusual about Mr. Chapin's room? Never mind describing your daily work there? What did you see that you didn't expect to see?"

"Well, sir, I saw a trunk and two bags all packed "

"Wait! How do you know they were packed? Did you look into them?"

"Oh, no, sor! I mean they were strapped and set side by side like they were to be taken away."

"And you think they contained Mr. Chapin's clothing?"

"I—think so. sir."

Jane shuddered and crossed herself. Clearly she had a fearsome, if undefined thought.

"Why do you think so?" went on Mr. Fiske.

"Because there was nothin' in the wardrobe or in the dresser drawers, and all his brushes and things was gone."

"You received the impression, then," said Mr. Fiske, "that Mr. Chapin had picked up his possessions during the night, with the intention of departure from White Birches?"

"It seemed that way to me, sir," said Jane, casting a troubled glance at Chapin, whose despairing aspect had not changed.

"But you then made up Mr. Chapin's room, as usual?"

"Yes, sir, just as usual."

"And when did you go to that room again?"

"Not until the next morning, sir. Peters looks after Mr. Chapin at night, sir."

"And the next morning were Mr. Chapin's trunks still packed?"

"No, sir; they had been taken away, and everything was put back in its place in the wardrobes and dresser."

"Apparently a change of plan," commented the coroner. "That will do, Jane; you're excused. Mr. Chapin, will you tell us why you packed up your belongings as if to go away?"

Ernest Chapin looked up with an effort. But in a steady, even voice he replied, "I did intend leaving here Tuesday morning, permanently."

"Because of your quarrel with Mr. Arnold?"

"As a result of that, yes."

The jurymen wagged their heads at one another by way of comment on this information.

"Why did you not carry out your intention, Mr. Chapin?"

"I learned Tuesday morning that Justin Arnold was missing, and I decided to stay until the mystery of his disappearance should be cleared up. As a matter of fact, Mr. Arnold and I severed our business relations during the interview I had with him."

"You mean, he discharged you from the post of secretary?"

"I mean exactly that." Chapin's voice had now assumed the dead tone of a man who has nothing more to hope for. Though his words were plausible, though his eyes were steady and frank, his voice and manner showed extreme dejection and a sort of final despair.

Without further consideration of Chapin's statements, Mr. Fiske called Peters, the valet. His evidence was the same as he had given before, with the exception of an added bit of information which seemed, to all the hearers, of decided importance.

"What do you know of Mr. Chapin's packed luggage? Did you pack for him?" said the coroner.

"No, sir."

"Did you unpack them?"

Peters fidgeted. He glanced at Chapin and seemed uncertain what to answer.

"Did you?" repeated the coroner, sternly.

"Yes, sir," Peters blurted out.

"When?"

"On Tuesday, about noon, Mr. Chapin asked me to do so. He said he had decided not to go away, and for me to put his clothes and things back in their places."

"Did he reward you for this?"

"Well, sir, he gave me a bit of a fee same as any gentleman would."

"A bit of a fee? How much?"

"A—a goodish bit, sir."

"Why a large fee?"

"Well, sir,—he—Mr. Chapin, he told me not to say anything about his having packed or unpacked."

"Not to say anything about it! To whom?"

"To anybody, sir."

"In a word," said the coroner, "Mr. Chapin bribed you to keep secret the facts that he had concluded to go away suddenly and had afterward changed his mind."

"If you put it that way, sir," agreed Peters.

"Have you any explanation to offer, Mr. Chapin, of these somewhat curious proceedings?" inquired the coroner.

But the worm had turned. Ernest Chapin sat bolt upright, his attitude became one of haughty indifference, and he said curtly, "I never make explanations concerning any fees I may choose to give servants."

"Then, let me ask you in a friendly way, Chapin," the coroner went on, in a somewhat gentler voice, "to give us any explanations that you will. For I may tell you frankly that what has been said here this morning seems to indicate that explanations must be required of you. It will be far wiser for you to volunteer them now than to be forced to give them later."

"I have none to give," said Chapin coldly. "I had no hand in the murder of Justin Arnold. I know nothing whatever about it. I had an unpleasant interview with him late Monday night, and when we parted, although we did so courteously, we were not good friends. But I did not kill him, nor have I the slightest idea who did."

The words were frank, the manner was sincere, and yet very few of those present believed Chapin's declaration. It was quite evident what the coroner thought.

"Mr. Chapin," he said, "I must warn you that you have made some very serious admissions. Without being more definite, I will say, that as you are the last man known to have seen Mr. Arnold, on the night he was killed, and as you have admitted quarrelling with him on that occasion, and as you have confessed to packing a large trunk that night, and bribing a servant to tell his own story of unpacking it, there is room for a theory that—"

But Ernest Chapin interrupted him. "That I secreted the dead body in my trunk! Mr. Coroner, your imagination is running away with you!"

"But we have only the word of a bribed servant and yourself that your clothing was in that trunk. It was a very strange performance, at best. A murderer could have secreted his victim's body in such a manner, and then, next day, when discovery threatened, transferred the body, still with the aid of that useful servant, to the place where it was eventually found."

To Dorothy, the white, fixed face of Chapin was but a proof of his horror at such a terrible charge. But to others it was the dismay and terror of a tracked criminal.

Then Chapin spoke. His voice was tense and strained, almost inaudible, and his lips quivered, but his words were clear.

"I have no reply to make to such a monstrous charge. It is for you to bring proof. Quiz Peters and see if you can get him to admit anything of the sort."

"Peters is in your pay, and is not likely to betray you. He has himself too much at stake to be trapped into an admission."

"Then do your worst!" cried Chapin, speaking now in a loud, defiant tone, and flashing angry glances round the room as well as at the coroner.

"I am not on trial for any part in or knowledge of Justin Arnold's death. Prove me guilty if you can!"

His voice rang out and he squared his shoulders with the air of one brought to bay, but determined to fight to the last. This attitude was not in his favor, and the coroner looked at him sternly, as he said, "That is all, Mr. Chapin."

CHAPTER 19: DOROTHY'S DISCLOSURES

THERE was an instant of quietness, and then there was almost a hubbub in the room. Several spoke at once, and the coroner was obliged to enforce order by rapping on the table.

As soon as quiet was restored, Dorothy spoke, and spoke rapidly and to the point.

"Mr. Coroner," she said, "have I a right to be heard?"

"Certainly, Miss Duncan, if you have any information to give concerning the case."

"I have." And then the girl's courage seemed to give out, and she sat, fingering her handkerchief, while every one, including Chapin, looked at her with breathless interest.

"Yes, Miss Duncan," said the coroner; "what is it?"

"Why, you see,—that is,—I didn't tell quite all the truth when I was questioned, but—but I will tell it now."

She waited so long before proceeding, that Fiske prompted her again; "And what is the truth, Miss Duncan?"

"Well, when I left Miss Duane's room on Monday night, I—I did not go directly to my own room, —I met Mr. Chapin in the hall, and I went with him out on the balcony for a few minutes."

"And then?"

"And then, Mr. Arnold came upstairs and he— he saw us and he was very, very angry, and he told me to go to my room."

"And did you?"

"Yes, but before I went, I heard him ask Mr. Chapin to go downstairs again with him, and Mr. Chapin did."

"And just why are you telling us this?"

"Because,—because, if those two men quarrelled, it was—it was about me." Dorothy looked adorable as she made this admission, and her big eyes turned to Chapin with a glance of hope that her story would in some way help him. "I think I ought to tell you, for Mr. Chapin refused to tell, simply for the sake of shielding me."

"Shielding you from what?"

Dorothy looked surprised. "Why, from the disgrace of being the subject of a quarrel. Any man would do that, if he were,—if he were fond of anybody."

This was more than Dorothy had meant to say, and she blushed hotly, while Chapin looked genuinely distressed.

"Go on," said the coroner, abruptly.

"That is all," said Dorothy, now very dignified; "I wish to relieve Mr. Chapin of any necessity of secrecy regarding the reason for his quarrel with Mr. Arnold."

The coroner looked thoughtful. "This, then, Mr. Chapin, was the cause of your quarrel with your employer, and the reason for his discharging you?"

"It was," returned Chapin frankly. "Since Miss Duncan has told you of the episode, I have no further reason to deny it. Mr. Arnold spoke to me in such a manner as might be expected of a jealous man. He was both just and generous, in the fact that he gave me a check for five thousand dollars in lieu of notice, and requested that I should leave White Birches at once. That is why I packed up on my return to my room. The next day, in view of his unaccountable disappearance, I deemed it best to stay here, in hope of being of some assistance."

The coroner looked but slightly impressed by these further disclosures, and said, "You say Mr. Arnold was both just and generous in his payment to you. Was he equally so in conversation?"

Chapin's face flushed. "He was not," he said. "On the contrary, he was both unjust and ungenerous in his words to me; but since he is not here to defend himself, I prefer to make no complaint of his attitude."

"Was not five thousand dollars a large sum to give you instead of the usual month's notice?"

Again Chapin flushed painfully. It seemed as if he were continually making ignominious admissions.

"The reason for so large a parting gift was because Mr. Arnold further informed me that he should erase from his will a bequest he had made to me."

"Oh, then, Mr. Arnold intended to cut you out of his will?"

"So he told me."

"But since he fortuitously died before he could carry out that intention, his bequest to you still stands in your name!"

"Oh, I say, that's too bad!" exclaimed Campbell Crosby, who was watching Chapin writhe under the scathing irony of the coroner.

"Thank you, Crosby," said Chapin, nodding at the young man gratefully; for it was the only hint of comradeship that had been given him during his ordeal.

"I cannot see, Mr. Chapin," said the coroner curtly, "that what Miss Duncan has told us, or what you have told us yourself, has any favorable bearing on the matter. Indeed, to my mind, you have simply added a plausible, if despicable, motive for wishing to be rid of Justin Arnold, before he should have opportunity to cut off your inheritance." Chapin simply looked at the man. He seemed to understand that words were useless, and he merely shrugged his shoulders and sat still.

And then Dorothy spoke again. "Mr. Coroner," she began.

"Yes, Miss Duncan; have you further disclosures to make?"

"Don't, Dorothy," said her mother, trying to calm the excited girl; "don't talk any more. Come away to your room. You need to rest."

"Rest, mother! when I can tell the real truth about this thing! No, I demand to be heard!" and Dorothy sat up very straight on the sofa while her mother's arm still encircled her. Her cheeks were burning, and her eyes shone like stars. Evidently she was keyed up for a great disclosure.

"I can prove to you," she said, speaking low-but rapidly, "that Ernest Chapin could have had no hand in this—this tragedy, because I, myself, saw Justin Arnold alive and well after Mr. Chapin left him."

"It is true, then, that you came downstairs at two o'clock as has been testified?" said Mr. Fiske.

"Not at two o'clock," corrected Dorothy, "but at a little after one. Whoever says I came down at two, is mistaken. I watched from my door to see Mr. Chapin come upstairs, and I saw him at just one o'clock."

"Did he see you?"

"No, I was peeping through the crack of my door. After he was out of sight, I crept downstairs to speak to Mr. Arnold. Surely I had a right to do so, as he was my fiance."

"We are not discussing your rights, nor the conventions," said Mr. Fiske, coldly; "what happened?"

"I had a short interview with Mr. Arnold and returned to my room."

"At what time?"

"At about half-past one."

The coroner turned to Mrs. Crane. "Did you not say you saw Miss Duncan go downstairs at two o'clock?"

"I did think so," replied Mabel Crane, "but I have since learned that my room clock was too fast, and it may well have been half an hour earlier."

"Go on," said the coroner to Dorothy.

"Well, that's all. I was with Mr. Arnold for half an hour after Mr. Chapin left him, which proves, you must admit, that Mr. Chapin did not kill him."

"What was the purport of your interview with Mr. Arnold?"

"I went down to ask him to overlook my offence, and be friends again."

"And was he willing to do so?"

"No!" and Dorothy looked enraged; "he was not. He told me he had discharged Mr. Chapin and I begged him to take him back, but he wouldn't."

"And you quarrelled?"

"We did."

"Did you break your engagement?"

Dorothy looked up, fearfully; "N—not exactly."

"What do you mean by not exactly?"

"I mean I offered to break it, but Mr. Arnold would not agree to that. But he scolded me so terribly that I—"

Everybody looked frightened, for all knew how Dorothy regarded scolding. Both Gale and Crosby remembered the night she had said she would kill Arnold if he scolded her. And both Gale and Crosby remembered the way she had pointed the dagger at Arnold in play, but with a very real significance.

Ernest Chapin stared at her, in a dazed sort, of way. He seemed to realize she was doing all this for him, and it fairly took his breath away.

"I protest!" he cried; "Miss Duncan must not be allowed to proceed with this testimony!"

"Lest she incriminate herself or you?" asked the coroner, unpleasantly.

"Neither! But Miss Duncan is under great stress of excitement, and is not altogether responsible for what she is saying."

"I am, too!" cried Dorothy, "and I insist on being heard."

"Proceed," said Mr. Fiske. "But it is only right, Miss Duncan, that I should warn you to be careful. Your story makes it appear that you were the last one to see Mr. Arnold alive."

"Yes, and so I was, until the murderer, whoever he was, came."

"Did you give Mr. Arnold a spray of scarlet sage?"

"No, I did not."

"You were wearing some in your belt?"

"Yes, but I didn't give him any then; nor did he have any when I saw him."

"Then you think the murderer brought it and placed it in his hand?"

Dorothy looked thoughtful. "I don't know," she said seriously; "that doesn't seem plausible, and yet, where could it have come from?"

"There was none in the room?"

"Yes. I think there was, in vases on the tables.

But Justin would scarcely break off a spray for himself after I left him."

"Not likely! Might he not have snatched a bit from your belt as you," the coroner drove the shaft home, "as you stabbed him with that dagger, in the mad passion of your rage?"

With a low moan, Dorothy fainted.

"Brute!" cried Leila Duane to the coroner, as Dorothy was carried from the room.

But Mr. Fiske was not to be stopped. "She incriminated herself!" he declared. "It has been told how Miss Duncan was inclined to use a dagger if she were scolded or chided; and, given desperate provocation and opportunity, she lost her head and struck what proved to be a fatal blow."

"You lie!" said Ernest Chapin. "I killed Justin Arnold, myself. I confess it. We quarrelled and I snatched up the dagger and drove it home. The rest you know."

"I do not believe you, Mr. Chapin," said the coroner, looking at him, intently. "I think you are saying that to shield Miss Duncan from suspicion. Or it may be you are an accessory after the fact. Did Miss Duncan strike the fatal blow, and, for of course she could not have carried the body down to the cellar, did she come to you for help?"

The cruel face of Mr. Fiske was aglow with excitement. He was a man who had no mercy, and once on a trail spared no one's feelings in his blunt questions.

Ernest Chapin was a big man, but he looked a veritable giant as he stood up and fairly thundered, "No! she did not! I tell you I killed Arnold, and I alone! Miss Duncan had gone upstairs after her interview with him, and I came down again to learn what had transpired. If he had been unjust or unkind to her, I was quite ready to kill him,—and did!"

"What magnificent lying!" exclaimed Campbell Crosby. "But totally unnecessary, my dear Chapin. We'll prove Dorothy's innocence without your perjury, noble though it is, in intent."

"That will do, Mr. Crosby," interposed the coroner; "I am conducting this case. Mr. Chapin, I accept your statements, for the moment, at least. Did you, by any chance, have a sprig of the red flower in your buttonhole?"

"I did," returned Chapin.

"Where did you get it?"

"Miss Duncan had given it to me earlier in the evening. In our struggle,—for there was a struggle, — Arnold grasped at the flower,—it had roused his jealousy in the first place,—and kept it clasped in his hand."

"Good Lord! What lying!" exclaimed Crosby.

"Did you do that, Dorothy?"

"Yes," said the girl. "But I gave a spray to Crane, too, and to Justin, so that counts nothing."

"What did Mr. Arnold do with the flower you gave him?" asked Fiske.

"He threw it away, he was so angry at me."

"Miss Duncan," said the coroner, very gravely, "you are not guilty of this murder, I am sure. But the evidence points strongly toward Mr. Chapin. And I feel sure you know all about the facts. Are you willing to tell truly what you know? There is no use in your making up falsehoods, for they will not be believed."

Dorothy stared at him a moment, her face white as chalk, and her eyes burning. Then she gave one quick glance at Chapin, and with a low, deep-drawn sigh, she again fainted; this time in her mother's arms—

CHAPTER 20: FLEMING STONE

WHAT happened just after that, Dorothy Duncan never quite knew. She knew that some dreadful officers took Ernest Chapin away, and she knew that they called it being arrested, but that it meant going to jail.

But with her returning senses came a realization of it all, and a mad, wild determination to conquer circumstances, to refute evidence, and to save Chapin yet. How this was to be accomplished, she had no idea, but never yet had Dorothy Duncan failed in an undertaking! To be sure, she had never undertaken such a task as this, but, on the other hand, she had never before felt the same power of strength and capability of endeavor. From a merry butterfly of a girl, she had suddenly bloomed into a singlehearted, loving woman, and she would save her love from his impending fate if a woman's will or a woman's wiles could do it!

Alone, in her own room, she came to these decisions, and went at once in search of definite advice. On the terrace she found Mr. Gale and Mr. Crosby.

"I want you to help me," she said simply, "both of you. In the first place, Ernest never killed Justin. I know he didn't, but I can't prove it to that horrid coroner man. Nor to that detective, either! He had a spite against Ernest from the very beginning."

"But, Miss Duncan," began Gale, "you must admit "

"I admit nothing! I know what you're going to say— 'circumstantial evidence,' and all that tomfoolery! I don't care for your opinion, Mr. Gale— pardon me if I am rude, but I mean exactly what I say! I'm not asking your opinion as to who killed Justin, for you don't know, and a mere opinion is worth nothing. What I ask you is this: can you direct me to the very best detective in the country? I don't mean what they call a central-office man; I mean a detective who can detect mysteries."

"Dorothy," said Crosby, looking at her closely, "don't talk like that; you are excited, child. You can do nothing in this matter. It is not work for a young girl."

"I'm a woman," said Dorothy, "and I demand consideration of what I have to say. You said yourself, Campbell, that you didn't believe Ernest committed the crime; now what are you going to do to find out who did do it, and save an innocent man?"

"There's Stone, of course," said Gale thoughtfully. "He's the only one, Dorothy, that I know of who can do miracles in detective work."

"Stone!" exclaimed Crosby. "Fleming Stone? For heaven's sake, don't get him!"

"Why not?" said Gale.

"In the first place, he never takes any but the most important cases; again he's outrageously expensive ; and, anyway, his services are so difficult to procure as to be practically impossible."

Dorothy looked at the speaker gravely. "Campbell, this is an important case. I'm sorry Mr. Stone's expensive, but I should think, as Justin's heir, you would be glad to spend your money toward the rightful avenging of his death! As to your third objection, that Mr. Stone's services are hard to obtain, I myself will engage to secure him for our case."

Gale looked in amazed admiration at this new Dorothy who had so suddenly come into being. Her beauty seemed intensified by the woman's soul that looked out of her eyes.

"By Jove! you're right!" exclaimed Gale, "Though I hate to believe it of Chapin, somehow I can't see any loophole for the man. And, Miss Duncan, if you want to appeal to the very highest possible talent in the detective line, go to Fleming Stone, and I'll warrant you'll persuade him to do your bidding. Shall I telephone him for you, and make an appointment at his place in New York? You never could see him any other way."

"Oh, do, please, Mr. Gale! I will keep any appointment he may make. Mother will go with me at any time to see him."

Gale went away on this errand, and Crosby turned suddenly to Dorothy, saying impulsively, "Don't let him do that, Dorothy! Run after him, and ask him not to telephone!"

"Why?" and Dorothy turned her large, sad eyes full on Crosby. "If you don't want to spend so much money, I will manage that part of it myself. Mother has some, and I have a little of my own."

"Don't talk like that, dearest! You know all that I have is yours, if you will accept it! Dorothy, will you promise to marry me if I will free Ernest Chapin from all suspicion of this crime?"

"Can you do that?"

"If I take the case, I can do it. I'd be a poor lawyer otherwise. But never mind that; will you promise to be mine if I succeed in setting Chapin free?"

Dorothy looked at him curiously. "If you can set him free, you must know something that you haven't yet told."

"Lawyers know lots of things they don't tell," said Crosby, almost flippantly; "but you haven't promised yet."

"Campbell," and Dorothy's piquant face was very sweet and serious as she spoke, "you may as well understand, once for all, that when Ernest Chapin is free, I shall marry him, and nobody else."

"Then I wash my hands of the whole affair," said Crosby angrily; "and a good time you and your precious Fleming Stone will have, trying to clear your lover! After you have failed, you may be glad to reconsider my offer."

"I may," said Dorothy, very gravely. "If Fleming Stone should fail, and if I were positive that you could free Ernest, I would consent to marry you —if you would not otherwise help him. But, Campbell Crosby, I would never marry you for any reason except to save Ernest Chapin's life!"

Dorothy turned and left him to such cold comfort as he might get from her parting speech. Going into the house, she met Gale, who said Mr. Stone was exceedingly sorry, but he was so busy it would be impossible for him to take up the case.

"Impossible!" cried Dorothy, in despair. "Oh, Mr. Gale, couldn't you persuade him?"

"No, I tried my best, but he wouldn't even consider it."

"Then that settles it," and Dorothy went on her way upstairs.

It was late evening now, but with firm step and determined air Dorothy went straight to a small telephone booth on the second floor. Finding the number in the book, she called up Fleming Stone. The great detective answered her kindly, when she made known her errand, but repeated his assertions of inability to take up the matter.

And now Dorothy Duncan called upon her uttermost powers of cajolery to help her persuade this man against his own will.

"Mr. Stone," she said in her most pleading voice, "won't you try to put yourself in my place for a moment? The man I love is in prison, under suspicion of a crime of which he is utterly innocent. Only you can save him for me. I am a naughty little girl, I have been called a coquette and a flirt all my life. Now has come my one love, the real love of my life. Must it be a tragedy? Won't you help me to save that man, to realize that love, and thereby make a woman, a true, loving woman, out of a foolish, frivolous madcap girl?"

"Miss Duncan, if I could arrange to do this thing, I would; but you must understand that other cases have prior claim on my time and attention. It wouldn't be just or right to neglect them."

"Mr. Stone," and Dorothy's voice was very sober, "did you never in all your life do a thing that was not just and right?"

"Why,—I think not willingly or premeditatedly."

"Then won't you, just this once? Oh, think what it means to me! Mr. Stone, did you ever love anybody?"

Fleming Stone hesitated a moment before he answered, slowly, "Yes."

And in that instant's hesitation Dorothy knew that her cause was won!

"Very, very much?" she said softly.

Again the hesitant "Yes."

"Then," and Dorothy showed no triumph in her voice, only pleading, "then, for her sake, won't you, oh, Mr. Stone, won't you help another woman?"

"I will," said Fleming Stone. "You have my promise, Miss Duncan, to do all I can for you. Can you come here to see me to-morrow morning? It will help to have an interview before I go to your place."

"Yes, I will be there. At what time?"

"Shall we say ten?"

"Very well; at ten o'clock. I will be prompt.

And—I thank you, Mr. Stone,—in her name."

Dorothy's tone was sweet and tender, and as Fleming Stone hung up his receiver, he fell into a reverie which lasted a long time, and whose visions were of a long time ago. Dorothy's instinct had led her to use the only argument that would have prevailed with Fleming Stone, and when he aroused himself from his waking dream, he found he would have to work nearly all night to complete some work that must be done if he were to accept this new commission.

Leaving the telephone table, Dorothy felt a strong desire to see no one, but to go straight to her room for the night. But she knew she must make arrangements for the trip to New York, so she went downstairs.

She told no one what persuasions she had used, but she told of her success in making an appointment with the famous detective.

"I'm mighty glad you've fixed it up," said Gale.

"Miss Duane and I have discussed the matter, and, though I frankly confess that things look very black for Chapin, we have felt that he should have the benefit of even a desire for doubt. And I assure you if Fleming Stone cannot find the criminal, no one can."

Dorothy remembered Campbell Crosby's offer to free Chapin himself, and concluded he meant to do it by legal chicanery; or else he merely made the rash promise in the hope of persuading her to marry him.

In one of the swift motor-cars belonging to the garage of White Birches, Dorothy and her mother started the next morning to see Mr. Stone. Leila had begged to go, too, saying that she would not ask to be present at the interview, but she wanted to see, at least, the reception-room of the great detective. Of course, Leila's going implied Gale's going also. So the four started off.

As in Gale's opinion it augured better success, Dorothy went into Mr. Stone's presence alone, leaving the others in the reception-room.

Dorothy felt no embarrassment or shyness as she went into the inner office, though office the room could scarcely be called. It was more like a great library, but with a cosy; pleasant air as of a room loved and lived in.

Fleming Stone regarded the girl with a grave interest. He made no reference to their conversation of the night before, and, taking the cue, Dorothy did not.

"Miss Duncan," said Stone, kindly, "what can I do for you?"

A week earlier Dorothy would have brought into play her whole bewitching paraphernalia of smiles, blushes, dimples, and long, drooping eyelashes. Now those wiles seemed to her trivial in the face of her great tragedy, and, dropping into the seat Mr. Stone placed for her, she looked straight in his face and said slowly, "You can do this for me, Mr. Stone. The man I hope to marry has been arrested for a murder he did not commit. But everybody believes he did it. Even the lawyers say there is no loophole for him."

"And you want me to find a loophole?" said Fleming Stone, smiling kindly at her as she paused.

"Oh, Mr. Stone, how good you are!" she cried, referring to his kindly tone and reassuring smile.

"No, I don't want you to find a loophole. I want you to find the man who did kill Mr. Arnold."

"And this man under arrest, your friend, is judged guilty, I suppose, because of circumstantial evidence so strong that it convinces everybody."

"Yes; but I know he didn't do it."

"And you have only that knowledge, as you term it, born of your affection for him, with which to refute this overwhelming tide of evidence?"

If Dorothy had faltered then, had hesitated, or had suddenly realized that her case was weak, she might not have roused Fleming Stone's interest. But she said simply, "Yes, Mr. Stone, that is all; but it is enough, for my knowledge is true, and the evidence is false—or not false, perhaps, but misleading."

"Give me a slight outline of the circumstances," said Fleming Stone, and, with a sigh of resignation, he pushed away the papers he had been working on and settled himself to listen.

Straightforwardly Dorothy told the story. She omitted no important detail, she did not gloss over the points that told against Chapin or herself, and she made no effort to cajole Fleming Stone's sympathy by any exhibition of sentiment or pathos.

He listened attentively, thought a few moments after she had finished, and then said:

"As part of our problem, then, we have first a house-party in a house that it is impossible to leave or enter during the night. We have a man who is in love with Mr. Arnold's fiancee. We have this man see Mr. Arnold at

night, when they engage in angry altercation. We find
Mr. Arnold dead the next morning. We know of no one
else who could have had any motive or opportunity for the
crime, and yet we are asked to prove that this man in
question did not do it."

Dorothy's heart fell like lead. The way in which Mr.
Stone set forth this sequence of arguments seemed to
point so indubitably to Chapin—or, at least, seemed to
prove that Mr. Stone thought they did—that Dorothy lost
all hope of his assistance.But she said bravely, though in
a faint voice,"Yes, that's what we have to prove."

"Plucky little piece," was Fleming Stone's inward
comment, but aloud he said, "Then, Miss Duncan, if that's
what we have to prove, the sooner we set about it the
better."

"Can you prove it, Mr. Stone?" and hope, suddenly
roused by his words, sent the color flying to Dorothy's
cheeks, the light to her eyes, and a tremulous smile to the
corners of her mouth.

Being merely human, after all, Fleming Stone caught
his breath at this sudden vision of animated beauty, but
he answered her query by saying, "You think Mr. Chapin
innocent, Miss Duncan?"

"I know him to be innocent, Mr. Stone."

"Then, you will not be so greatly surprised when I say
I agree with you."

CHAPTER 21: THE KEY OF THE MYSTERY

DOROTHY gave a rapturous, almost inarticulate gasp, and, jumping up, impulsively held out two little roseleaf hands that were as impulsively clasped by Fleming Stone.

"You dear man!" she breathed, and the glory in her eyes seemed to dart far beyond the enclosing walls of the room, penetrating, Stone felt sure, even to the cell where her lover sat.

Unconscious, in her joy, of having acted unconventionally, Dorothy resumed her seat, and Fleming Stone took up the conversation.

"It seems a baffling case," he said, "and doubtless you are too inexperienced to know that often the baffling cases solve themselves more readily than the simpler ones. To begin with, Miss Duncan, I ignore all suspicion of you, either as accessory or as having any guilty knowledge of the affair. I am positive you know no more than you have so frankly told me."

"Why are you so sure?" Dorothy asked the question simply.

"Because I can read you and because it would be absurd for you to seek my services, if there were any danger of finding evidence against you."

And Fleming Stone's glance gave Dorothy an unspoken assurance that he knew no guilty person could have spoken to him as she did over the telephone.

"Your play with the dagger is meaningless," he went on. "As you said, you have a foolish attraction toward the picturesque weapon, but I am sure I am safe in saying you are cured of that."

A sad little smile confirmed this statement, and Stone went on. "You left Mr. Arnold alive and well, just as you have said; and, tell me, was he wearing a boutonniere of the scarlet sage?"

"No, Mr. Stone. I had given him one earlier in the evening, but he had thrown it away."

"You had given Mr. Chapin one?"

"Yes; but, Mr. Stone, I have given them to all the men all the week. I decorated Mr. Crane every day. Also Mr. Gale and Mr. Crosby. When they went away on Monday, I gave them each a sprig; and I even gave old Dr. Gaspard one. It is my favorite flower, and I almost always wear it when it is in season."

"Then it may not be a definite clue. I think, Miss Duncan, the strongest argument against your faith in Mr. Chapin is his speech, of which you told me yourself: that he said he didn't care what had become of Mr. Arnold, and that he would be willing to commit crime to win you."

Dorothy hesitated a moment, then she blushed a rosy red, and, as if with sudden determination, she said, "But, Mr. Stone, Mr. Crosby said that, too. He said he didn't care what had become of Justin if it left me free to marry him. I know these are awfully conceited things for a girl to tell, but I'm only trying to show you that a man doesn't always mean the desperate things he says."

"Miss Duncan," said Stone, "I may as well confess I brought up that point to see if you would not answer it in some such manner as you did. I feel sure you have had a wide and varied circle of admirers, and I know you have learned not to take all their remarks too literally. I'm making this point because I want you to understand that I do not really consider that speech of Mr. Chapin's as evidence against him. On the contrary, if a man has murder in his heart, he's most careful, usually, not to let such a thing creep into his speech. Now, another point, the fact that Mr. Chapin packed up his clothing at night, after being discharged by his employer, and unpacked it again the next day, is to my mind distinctly in his favor.

Whatever was his condition of mind when he packed his boxes after his angry interview with Mr. Arnold, it was changed when he learned that Mr. Arnold had disappeared. Had he been the cause of that disappearance, he would not have been surprised at the information, and would have had no reason to change his plans accordingly."

"That is true!" cried Dorothy excitedly. "That horrid coroner was bound to suspect Ernest, and he made every bit of evidence seem to be against him, whether it was or not."

"It is a common mistake to theorize, and then insist on fitting the facts to one's theory. Miss Duncan, "I cannot promise you success, but I can promise you my best endeavors to fasten this crime where it rightly belongs, and I do not think now that the criminal's name is Chapin."

"Who do you think did it?" asked Dyrothy quickly.

"I haven't an idea, though I have the least little, tiny glimmering of a direction in which to look. Further than that, I cannot say, until I can go to White Birches and examine the scene of the crime."

"But it is too late to find clues! To-day is Friday— that's four days since—since it happened."

"Some clues are ineffaceable," said Stone gravely. "A living clue is not lost sight of in four days."

Suddenly Dorothy felt enveloped in the mystery of this man's genius. He knew nothing of the case save what she had told him. She had told him nothing of the case save what had been heard by the jury who had convicted Chapin; and yet here was this man implying that he considered Ernest innocent, and talking about living clues, as if he already had the criminal in mind!

"When will you come, Mr. Stone?"

"I will go to White Birches to-morrow morning, and remain there, if necessary, over the week-end."

"And"—Dorothy hesitated, and stammered a little— "but—they tell me you are very expensive, Mr. Stone."

"Much depends on circumstances, Miss Duncan. If Mr. Chapin is freed, perhaps he will pay my not exorbitant fee out of his legacy."

Dorothy looked pained for a moment, and then she realized that if Ernest were freed, and the real criminal discovered, there could be no stigma attached to the bequest of Arnold.

After the briefest of good-byes, Mr. Stone held the door open for her, and closed it immediately after her, so that Leila caught not even a glimpse of the celebrated detective.

"'But you will see him, Leila, you will!" exclaimed Dorothy, as she threw her arm around her mother's neck, in her gladness. "Oh, Mother, he's coming to-morrow, and he knows Ernest didn't kill Justin, and he's going to find out who did—though I think he knows that, too, already!"

"By Jove, Dorothy, you're a wonder!" exclaimed Emory Gale, "You must have hypnotized him to think just what you wanted him to! I didn't think he was that sort of man!"

"He isn't that sort of man," said Dorothy, smiling happily. "He just thinks his own thoughts, but he thinks Ernest is innocent, and he's going to make everybody else think so, too."

Fleming Stone arrived Saturday morning. His winning personality appealed to them all, and though Leila was surprised that the great detective should have the polished manner of the men of her own world, she, with the others, fell under the thrall of his personal magnetism.

Mr. Stone did not desire the household to come together, so that he might ask them questions officially. Instead, he wandered about the house and grounds, conversing casually with the different ones, and seemingly going about at random.

In fact, Emory Gale began to think that the man's powers had been overrated, and that he was floundering, because he knew not in which direction to look.

Fred Crane was secretly disgusted at the detective's methods; but Miss Abby Wadsworth sniffed openly, and said to Mrs. Duncan that for her part she thought Mr. Wheeler had twice the brains of Mr. Stone.

The detective whom she thus flattered, however, was of quite another mind. James Wheeler, who had begged to be present, appreciated what Fleming Stone was doing. He followed the great man about, furtively watching every expression of his face and every direction of his eyes. He listened to Mr. Stone's remarks—noting the vital questions veiled by casual effects—and almost held his breath as he endeavored to trace the workings of the subtle mind. Fleming Stone was especially interested in the great wall and the gates that guarded White Birches from intrusion.

"Can we find no loophole?" he asked as he searched the whole place.

"No," cried Fred Crane exultantly; "I have been round and round the wall, inside and out, and there is no way a man could get under or over or through!"

"What's this?" and Stone picked up a small key from the ground, quite near the wall.

With the detective were Fred Crane, Mr. Wheeler and Malony. They all examined the key.

"There's no doubt as to what it is," said Wheeler, "it's a prestolite key. But where did it come from, and how did it get here?"

"What's a prestolite key?" asked Crane, who was not a motorist.

"A key to turn on the big motor searchlights that illumine the path ahead at night," answered Stone.

"Does it belong to you, Malony?"

"No, sor," and the old Irishman shook his head; "we have a different shtyle from the likes o' thot. But how the divil, savin' yer prisince, sor, cud thot thing iver get inside these walls?"

"That's the question," said Stone; "a motor could scarcely leap the wall and drive about the grounds."

"Do they use such a key in an aeroplane?" inquired Wheeler, who had been secretly nursing an airship theory for some time.

"I think not," returned Stone, who was gazing absently at the key and then at the wall. "Curious to find it so near the wall, eh?"

Both Wheeler and Crane were overjoyed at the attitude of the famous detective, who seemed to defer to them at every turn.

As a matter of fact, it was only seeming, for Fleming Stone kept his real thoughts to himself, and made unimportant speeches to occupy his hearers' attention while he was thinking.

He put the key in his pocket, and said in a most serious way: "I charge you strictly, gentlemen, to say nothing of this key to anyone. It may be of no importance as a clue, but I fancy it is, and I must ask your promise to divulge to no one,—no one at all, the fact of its being found. You hear, Malony?"

"Yis, sor. I'll say nothin'. But, sor, av ye plaze, where did it come from?"

"I don't know yet, for sure, Malony, but I think we shall find out soon."

After not more than an hour at White Birches, Mr. Stone went away for an interview with Ernest Chapin. At her earnest request, Dorothy was allowed to accompany him.

The interview was brief but very much to the point.

"Mr. Chapin," said Fleming Stone, "I am going to begin by assuming that you are innocent of this crime. But I should like your statement to that effect."

"You shall have it," and Chapin spoke frankly, looking Stone square in the eye. "I am innocent.

Entirely so. I said I was guilty to shield Miss Duncan from a possible suspicion which seemed to me to be hovering very near her."

"You yourself did not believe Miss Duncan could be guilty?"

"I cannot tell you. I could not believe it in my heart, for I love her too deeply; but I knew her quick impulsive nature, I knew her strange infatuation for sharp weapons, and I knew her especial aversion to being scolded. With this knowledge, while I could not and did not think her guilty, I had to admit to myself the possibility of it; or at least, I thought I did. And rather than run the slightest risk of her being suspected, I willingly shouldered the crime. Now that you have come, I am sure the truth will be brought to light, and so I declare myself innocent."

"You had a stormy interview with Mr. Arnold?"

"It was, indeed. He was justly incensed because the woman he loved had given her heart to me, and he had discovered it. I do not blame him for feeling as he did. I was not very honorable and my only excuse is that Miss Duncan did love me, and so blinded my honor, my judgment, and my loyalty to my employer. For many years Mr. Arnold had been most kind to me, and I did illy repay him to treat him as I did."

"Your words are true, Mr. Chapin, but that is all past now, and so beyond ethical argument. It is to be hoped that you and Miss Duncan have yet many years of happiness in store, and to gain that, we must first discover the murderer of Justin Arnold."

"Have you any suspicion as to the identity of the criminal, Mr. Stone?"

Fleming Stone did not answer this direct question, but said: "At what time did you leave Mr. Arnold?"

"At about one o'clock," replied Chapin.

"And you went downstairs, Miss Duncan?"

"At about ten minutes after one. I saw Mr. Chapin come up, and waited for him to get to his room. I went down, partly to make peace with Mr. Arnold, and partly to learn what he had said to Mr. Chapin."

"Then you went back upstairs at what time?"

"At about half-past one; perhaps twenty minutes of two."

"You saw no one about?"

"No."

"Did either of you hear Mr. Arnold come upstairs?"

"Why, no," returned Chapin; "as the presumption is he never came up."

"Did you hear any noise during the rest of the night?"

"No," said Dorothy, but Ernest Chapin said: "I heard some sounds, which I assume to be the rats in the wall that the servants mentioned."

"Tell me of these sounds," said Stone with greatest interest.

"It was, I think, a little before two o'clock," said Chapin. "I had not been to sleep, and I heard a sound in the wall at the head of my bed, a sort of scratching sound as of something going up or down. When the servants spoke of rats, I decided that was what it was, though I had never heard them before. The sounds ceased, and I fell into a restless doze, when I was awakened by a repetition of the same or similar sounds. I looked at my watch and it was then about three o'clock. I heard no more of them, but I was then so thoroughly wide awake I couldn't lie still, so I got up and packed my clothing and belongings. Mr. Arnold had discharged me from my position as his secretary, but he hadn't told me to leave at once. However, I felt I could not stay, and decided to leave early the next morning. When I learned of Mr. Arnold's strange disappearance, I concluded to stay until the mystery was cleared. So I told Peters to unpack my things. I did give him a fee, as has always been my habit when he did extra services for me, and I did ask him not to mention the matter; but the two incidents had no connection, and it was not a case of bribery as has been charged."

"I believe you implicitly, Mr. Chapin," said Stone; "what interests me most is those strange sounds in the wall. Why should rats appear suddenly, when you have never heard them there before?"

"I don't know, I'm sure," said Chapin, wearily, "but I can't see that it has any bearing on the crime. No secret passage exists in that wall or any other, for I have examined the house myself, aside from the searchings of the detective and Mr. Crane and the others."

"Thank you, Mr. Chapin," said Fleming Stone, as he left. "You have helped me more than you know. I feel sure we shall unravel this tangled thread of mystery in a few days, at most. Come, Miss Duncan, are you ready to go?"

But even as he spoke, Fleming Stone turned aside to give the pair an opportunity for a word alone, and at his nod the warden also waited a moment. And then the two visitors went away, and Chapin was left in his cell, but with a heart full of hope and faith in the great detective's powers.

Stone helped Dorothy into the car and got in beside her. She looked at him appealingly; he replied at once to her unspoken question.

"Your faith is not misplaced, my dear child. Mr. Chapin is innocent of the crime; and though he must remain where he is until the criminal is discovered, it is fortunate that he has the knowledge of your love and loyalty to cheer him. Moreover, he may yet owe his very life to your insistence on his innocence; for I have never seen a more convincing pile of circumstantial evidence against an innocent man."

"But how are you going to find the culprit, Mr. Stone?"

"There seems to be no direction in which to look. There are, in fact, very few directions in which to look; but I'm sure you can understand that the very limitations of the outlook must mean quick work."

Dorothy didn't quite understand this, but as Mr. Stone became silent and seemed lost in thought, she said nothing further to him.

CHAPTER 22: THE WHITE ALLEY

ONCE again at White Birches, Mr. Stone went systematically to work. He asked for a footman to lead him to such portions of the house as he wished to visit. But it was all done so quietly and unostentatiously that most of the household returned to their own interests and paid no attention to the wanderings of erratic genius.

Mr. Wheeler followed close in the footsteps of Fleming Stone, while Dorothy hovered in the background, eagerly awaiting some development that she might understand.

Stone went at once to the roofs, and glanced about at the trap-doors and scuttles in much the way Wheeler had done before him, thereby causing the heart of the lesser detective to swell with pride.

When Stone opened the scuttle that led to the small dark attic in the old ell, Mr. Wheeler remarked,

"There's no use looking in there, Mr. Stone. That little loft has no outlet into the house. Its only door has been nailed up for years."

"Thank you," said Fleming Stone, who had already half disappeared through the scuttle. He went on down and remained in the attic for several minutes, and, after returning to the roof, reentered the house by the trap-door through which they had come up.

Stone's manner had changed somewhat. Though not discourteous in anyway, he was so absorbed in his own thoughts as to seem oblivious to all about him. Descending from one story to another, he paused at certain rooms and looked in. It was an old part of the house, occupied mostly by the servants.

He next asked to speak with Jane and Peters, whose bedrooms he had noticed especially.

"You remember the night your master disappeared?" he asked abruptly of the two servants.

"Yes, sir," they replied.

"Did you hear any noise at all during the night?"

"No, sir."

"Not any noise at all? No usual noises?"

"Well, sir," said Jane, "there was the rats in the wall, sir."

"And most uncommon bad they was that night, sir," added Peters reminiscently.

"Ah!" and Fleming Stone seemed deeply interested in the information. "And do you often hear rats in the wall?"

"Now and again, sir; but that night they was worse than usual. This is a very old part of the house, sir, and we can't seem to get altogether rid of them."

"That will do."

Mr. Wheeler noticed the gleam in Fleming Stone's eye, and felt sure that however inexplicable it might be, the rats in the wall had to do with the mystery of White Birches!

Next Fleming Stone went straight to the cellar, with the footman leading the way, and the faithful Wheeler and the eager Dorothy following. Stone carefully examined the old oven and the various small rooms in that part of the cellar. An old work-bench stood against a white-washed brick wall. This he pulled away, disclosing an opening into a space behind the chimney. Though thick with dust and dirt and cobwebs, Mr. Stone peered into it, and, stooping, picked up a pocket-knife, which he pocketed without a glance. With a stick, he poked around in the accumulated rubbish, and gave a sudden exclamation as he picked up a small white marble. He gazed at it a moment with intense concentration, and then, turning, he offered it to Dorothy.

"There's the clue," he said exultantly.

"What is it?" inquired the girl, as she took the marble, wonderingly.

"It is a white alley."

"What is it for?"

"It was made for boys to play with; but its present use is to clear your lover from the unjust charge hanging over him. His is a narrow chance, but he will yet make it. You'd better preserve that white alley, for the time will come when you will realize its importance."

Though she fought against the conviction, Dorothy couldn't help an impression that Fleming Stone was crazy. But James Wheeler stood as one enthralled. Here was detective work such as he had dreamed of but never accomplished! To pick up a common marble, a boy's marble, of the type called an alley, and by its aid to discover the man who killed Justin Arnold—this was wonderful work indeed! Not spectacular—Fleming Stone could not be that—but an exhibition of the deduction made by genius from logical observation and inference.

"How did it get there?" inquired Dorothy, for lack of a more intelligent question to ask. "It has probably been there for twenty years," replied Stone carelessly, and with this unilluminating speech he turned and went upstairs.

Mr. Stone seemed to look upon Miss Wadsworth as the head of the somewhat disintegrated household, and he at once sought her presence.

"I have to go away now," he said to her. "I have done all that can be accomplished here at present."

"But you have been here barely three hours, Mr. Stone."

"Much may be done in a short time if that time be not wasted. I must go now, but I will return Monday morning, and I expect then to give you the result of my inquiries into this case."

"Will you not stay to luncheon?" Miss Abby spoke coldly, for she did not believe Mr. Stone had accomplished anything, and thought he only wanted to get away.

"No, thank you. If you will send me back to New York in the motor, I shall be glad to go at once."

Though they did not know it, the very fact that Fleming Stone's manner was a shade less affable than usual was really a tribute to the fact that he was deeply engrossed in the case.

Only to Dorothy did he smile, when he bade her good-by, and said kindly, "Keep up a good heart, little girl. It will all come out right for you and your lover, but the disclosure of the truth will be a sad event for all."

"Well, for a story-book detective, he's the right sort," said Campbell Crosby, with a supercilious laugh; "but they don't amount to much when it comes to solving a real mystery."

"I think he will solve it," said Dorothy; "and he's coming back Monday to tell us."

"Where is he going in the meantime, Dorothy?" said Crosby. "You seem to be in his confidence more than the rest of us."

"I don't know, Campbell; but I don't think it has anything to do with this case. He's an awfully busy man, and I think he has put us off until Monday so he can attend to something else."

"I don't think so," volunteered Mr. Wheeler.

"I think he's pretty much interested in this case, and I think that, wherever he's going, it is on business connected with it'."

"I don't," said Miss Abby disdainfully. "I think he's gone off somewhere to a week-end party; and I doubt if we ever see him again!"

But Miss Wadsworth was wrong, for on Monday morning Fleming Stone reappeared. He was courteous and charming, but exceedingly grave.

He asked the members of the household and the guests to assemble in the library, but he advised that the servants be excluded.

"I have discovered," Mr. Stone began, "to my own satisfaction, the assassin of Justin Arnold. But I will tell you the reasons I have for my opinion, and you may conclude for yourselves if I am right. As you know, a seemingly inexplicable problem confronted us. It appeared that the man who killed Justin Arnold could not have gained entrance to White Birches that night. This was based on the assumption that no entrances were known except the ordinary ones. A search was made to find such an entrance, but it was stopped too soon. Such an entrance exists, and was used. Another direction in which to look is the old principle of seeking him whom the crime will benefit; this too was also done to a degree, but again the search stopped too soon. Let us reconstruct the situation. Mr. Arnold is left alone in his library, late at night. His secretary left him at one o'clock, and Miss Duncan a half hour later. By, let us say, half-past one or soon thereafter, the entire household was asleep, save Mr. Arnold. We may assume this since he apparently did not go to his bedroom at all. Let us, then, picture an intruder, who enters the house, goes directly to Mr. Arnold in the library, and, after we know not what sort of an interview, stabs him, prevents incriminating evidence of his deed by the use of a pillow hastily snatched from a nearby couch, and then carries the dead body of his friend to the cellar."

"Why do you say friend, Mr. Stone?" asked Mr. Wheeler, who had been listening intently.

"Had it been other than a friend, Mr. Arnold would have raised an outcry. I said an intruder, but I did not say a marauder. It must have been a man whose unexpected appearance may have surprised but did not alarm Mr. Arnold."

"And how did this intruder effect this entrance?" inquired Campbell Crosby, thus voicing the question in everybody's mind.

"By means of the secret entrance of which I spoke."

"There is no sliding panel or secret stairway in this house," declared Crosby, in tones of certainty.

"Not a secret passage of the sort built in old castles," said Fleming Stone quietly, "but, none the less, a secret mode of entrance, unused for years and almost undiscoverable. Suppose I tell you how I found it. It was through the process of elimination. Your really thorough search for such a means of entrance, I found, omitted only one thing; and that was an exploration of the attic over the old ell. I believe you looked down through the scuttle, but did not go in. Clearly, it was the only place left to search, so I searched it. I found footprints in the dust on the old floor, which, though of no especial use for identification, proved that someone had been there recently. As you said, there is no outlet from that attic into the house, the door being nailed up. But as I stood there, looking about by the light of my pocket electric, I noticed, besides the dry garret smell, the characteristic damp odor of the cellar. I found it came up back of the chimney. Investigation proved that the chimney, probably as a precaution against fire, had been built more than a foot away from the external wall of the house. This space or shaft, I concluded, must descend unimpeded to the cellar, to account for that dampness and odor. As a test, I dropped my pocket knife in it and heard it strike down below. I then turned to the roof, and traced the direction of the shaft down through each story. On reaching the cellar, I found, as I had expected, that this vacant space behind the brick chimney extended directly from cellar to attic I found, moreover, large nails driven zigzag into the old wooden joists, by means of which an agile person could climb up if he desired. I picked up my pocket knife—which had proved the directness of the shaft — and, poking about in the rubbish, I found a white alley. This seemed to me to prove my theory that at some time, years ago, boys used to hide here during their play in the old cellar. I had now found how the intruder could get in and out of the house— if he knew of this shaft. Which knowledge, by the way, would imply that he was one of the boys who used to play in this cellar. By inquiring of the servants, I learned that they heard, or thought they heard, unusually loud noises that night, made by the rats in the walls. These unusual noises I take to be due to the entrance and exit of the intruder, through the shaft behind the chimney, by means of the long nails protruding from the joists—in exactly the same fashion as when he was a boy."

There was intense silence in the room. No one looked at anyone else, each seemingly unwilling to breathe the first suggestion of suspicion.

But James Wheeler, absorbed in the technical words of the detective, said breathlessly, "But how did the intruder get up to the roof of the house, to enter at this scuttle? And, before that, how did he get over the wall into the grounds?"

"Remember, Mr. Wheeler, that if my theory is the right one, this intruder, when a boy, playing with marbles, must have been familiar with every inch of the house and grounds. Moreover, if he made his entrance and exit by that shaft of which I have told you, it presupposes a man—for that boy must now be a man—of unusual ingenuity, agility, athletic strength, and daring. I cannot tell you all the details of his entrance from the outer world, but I can give you enough of them to support my claims to plausibility. To begin, the intruder arrived outside the wall, let us say, not long after one o'clock. He brought with him, by way of paraphernalia, a slight rope-ladder, made of fine, strong fish-line. Also a ball of fine fish-line and a weight, very likely a fishline sinker. Outside the wall, but near it, there is a tree whose spreading branches should have been trimmed away by people as cautious as the Arnold family. But I understand that their excessive precaution is largely tradition, and so this tree has been allowed to grow until it offers a fine point of vantage for one who wishes to note the movements of the watchman, Malony. Our intruder, let us say, climbed this tree and awaited such a time as the watchman should be at his most distant point. Then, still from the branches of the tree, he throws down a piece of rope-ladder or knotted rope inside the wall at the top, hooking it over the sharp points of broken glass and mortar. He then calmly places a board on these otherwise impassable points—I know this because I have since examined the board—and climbs down his rope-ladder or knotted rope inside the wall. This contrivance he leaves on the wall, as there is no fear of its detection in the darkness. He goes to the house and unrolls a much longer rope-ladder of the same sort. To this is attached his ball of fish-line and sinker. With a good aim he throws the sinker over the low ell of the house. Going around the house and picking up the sinker, he proceeds to pull the line up over the ridge-pole till the ladder reaches the roof, and then fastens his line to a veranda pillar."

"Do you know he did this?" asked Campbell Crosby quietly.

"I know he did this," returned Fleming Stone, as quietly, "because I found the mark in the turf where the weight struck it; I found a very little fresh dirt near the veranda post; and I also found an end of the fish-line left in the carving of the pillar, where it had hastily been cut off short. On the other side of the house I found many scratches on the painted clapboards, where the intruder had climbed his ladder, up the side of the house.

"To resume, after climbing his ladder to the roof, he goes in through the scuttle; down through the shaft, and up the cellar-stairs, to Justin Arnold's library. After accomplishing his premeditated and fiendish purpose, he disposes of the body of his friend, climbs the shaft, and retraces his steps to the wall and over it. As his ingenious rope-ladders, or whatever he may have used, have not been found, we may conclude he carried them away with him; but the board that assisted him over the wall, he was thoughtless enough to toss into some high grass nearby, and that has been found."

"You looked for it?" exclaimed Mr. Wheeler, with staring eyes.

"I instructed a gardener to look for it, and he found it. Now, granting all this, it only remained to find out who this intruder was, and where he came from. A few odd hints here and there had given me a suspicion and I set to work on it. The finding of the prestolite key proved the real key to the puzzle. This key," and Fleming Stone took it from his pocket, "I found on the ground near the wall and near that part of the wall where I discovered the intruder had entered. Therefore, I felt sure our man had come in an automobile, and having this key in his pocket he had lost it while climbing the wall. That climb was not an easy one at best, and a small key could very well have slipped out of a coat pocket."

"Let me see the key," said Emory Gale, and it was handed to him.

He looked at it a moment and handed it back without a word.

"As I told you," resumed Stone, "my suspicions had been aroused in a certain quarter, and implicated a man in a motor-car. But where could he leave his car while entering this place by means of the wall? There is no public garage very near, so I assumed he left his car at a garage in New York City, and came up here by subway or elevated railroad. At any rate, I worked along this line. I did not search the city garages, but further assuming that the man must needs cross the ferry to New Jersey on his return trip, I reasoned that he would not miss his key until on the Jersey side, or at least on the ferryboat. For it is not allowed to show those blinding, brilliant lights in the limits of the city, but immediately on striking the country roads they are necessary."

"The Jersey roads, you said?" and Fred Crane leaned forward in his eagerness.

"Yes, the man started for New Jersey, but his destination was beyond that State. I crossed the ferry myself, assuming that as soon as the missing key was needed, the owner would stop at some garage, and buy or borrow one. Nor was I mistaken. At the third place I inquired, I learned that a motorist did stop at about four o'clock Tuesday morning and ask for the use of a key to turn on his lights, saying he had lost his own."

"You got a description of this man?" asked Detective Wheeler.

"Certainly. An unmistakable description. He stayed but a moment and then went on; but his own description and that of his car can be verified by the garage keeper at any time. I have nothing more to add, as I think it unnecessary to say the name of the one who benefits most in a mercenary way by this crime; the one who has been familiar with this whole place from boyhood; and the one who is athletic, of strong, wiry build, and possessed of the cool daring and ingenuity required to carry out such an enterprise."

CHAPTER 23: CONFESSION

THOUGH Campbell Crosby's face was white and set, it was with rage, not fear.

"How dare you!" he exclaimed, as he fairly glared at Fleming Stone. "It is impossible to ignore the fact that your dastardly accusations are directed toward me! And I would deny them, but for the fact that they are so ridiculously absurd as to need no denial! I am disinclined even to take up the subject with you. But I will tell you, what every one else present knows, that my connection with this case in any way is an utter impossibility! The night it occurred I was in Philadelphia. I left White Birches at noon the day before my cousin disappeared, and I returned in the evening of the day after he disappeared."

"And you can give an account of yourself, Mr. Crosby, during that interval of absence?" Fleming Stone's eyes had lost all their softness now. They gleamed with stern justice as he looked at Campbell Crosby, and they glittered ominously as Crosby replied:

"Every moment of it! My partner, Mr. Gale, is present and he will vouch for the truth of my statements. Though the audacity of your accusation makes me wish to treat it with the silent contempt it deserves!"

Emory Gale looked bewildered. "I cannot understand it at all, Mr. Stone," he said. "Mr. Crosby was in my company almost continuously from the time we left White Birches until we returned here together."

"Almost continuously, Mr. Ga-le," repeated Fleming Stone gravely. "What were the hours that Mr. Crosby was not in your company?"

"Why, let me see. Only during the night, I think. We reached Philadelphia about six, dined separately, and were to meet later, but Crosby concluded to go to a concert, so I didn't see him again until he came to the office next morning at the usual time."

"Then you saw him, let us say, at six o'clock Monday night, and next at nine o'clock Tuesday morning?"

"Approximately that."

"And between those hours, Mr. Gale, Mr. Crosby returned to White Birches, accomplished what he came for, and went back again to Philadelphia, in time to reach the office as usual."

"You lie!" exclaimed Campbell Crosby, springing from his seat.

"No, I speak the truth, Mr. Crosby, and I must ask you to discuss the matter more quietly."

"But, Mr. Stone," went on Emory Gale, looking puzzled, "there must be a mistake somewhere, for Cam telephoned me two or three times Monday evening; the last time just as I was retiring, at about eleven-thirty o'clock. It would be a physical impossibility for him to make the trip from Philadelphia to New York, visit White Birches, and get back again to Philadelphia between eleven-thirty at night and seven in the morning, for he telephoned me at seven o'clock in the morning regarding a bit of special business."

"Yes, that's what it would be, a physical impossibility!" agreed Mr. Wheeler, counting the hours on his fingers.

"Mr. Crosby did not accomplish a physical impossibility," said Fleming Stone. "Where was he when he telephoned you at eleven-thirty o'clock, Mr. Gale?"

"At his hotel."

"How do you know he was there?"

"He said so."

"Ah, he was not quite truthful. As a matter of fact, he telephoned you at eleven o'clock on Monday night from Newark, New Jersey. I know, for I have verified the long-distance call."

Perhaps not so much because of what Fleming Stone said, as because of the calm certainty with which he said it, Campbell Crosby gave up.

"You have beaten me," he said to Mr. Stone. "I did concoct and carry out a plan exactly as you have described it. But I am too clever not to realize when I am cornered. My dear friends "—and Crosby glanced round the room—" Mr. Fleming Stone is right. I could, supply to his story a few missing details concerning that midnight trip, in a high-powered runabout. I could tell you of the annoying delays in getting long-distance telephone connections, and waiting for infrequent subway trains. But Mr. Stone has given you the main truths of what happened. He cannot know, nor can anyone who did not hear it, the provocation I received from Justin Arnold that night. I came here intending to kill him, if he would not give up to me the girl who had promised to marry him, although she did not love him. He told me that he had about decided himself, that he would allow her to break the engagement, as she had very shortly before told him she wanted to, but, since my request, he had changed his mind and should hold her to her promise. That enraged me, and I told him just what I thought of him. Also he told me what he thought of me, and they were not, either of them, beautiful thoughts. I had in my coat a sprig of scarlet sage which Dorothy had placed there when I went away at noon. It was faded, but I cherished it. Justin knew where I got it, and took it from me. That was the last straw! I fought him for it, but he held it tight in his hand, where it was,—at last,—found. In a blind fury I grabbed up the dagger, intending merely to threaten him, but he taunted me too far,—and the thing happened. I don't attempt to justify my deed, but neither do I regret it. Justin Arnold was not a good man and could never have made any woman happy. He was—"

Suddenly Crosby's bravado broke down. With a pathetic gesture of utter despair, he looked straight at Dorothy, and said, "But, Dorothy, I did it all for you.

Perhaps you other men cannot understand what it means to love a girl enough to commit a crime for her. Perhaps your finer natures would not feel that crime could result from intense and passionate love. But in my case it did. Ever since Dorothy became engaged to Justin Arnold, I've wanted to kill Justin Arnold. I've lived for it, and toward it. He had everything, and I nothing. He had fortune, home, leisure, and added to those he had the promise erf the girl I love! I tried not to do this thing; I had long talks with Justin, begging him to give up Dorothy, who never loved him. Had he spoken kindly to me, or even frankly, as man to man, it might have been different. But he taunted me with my poverty, with laziness, and with general undesirableness. He even dared me to go ahead and win Dorothy from him if I could, saying he knew I could not, because I had no money. With his death, his money would all be mine, also his home, and also —as I firmly believed—the girl that we both wanted. The consequences you know. The further consequences you will now learn. I have made a will— for I suppose that at the present moment the estate of the late Justin Arnold is legally mine. At my death it will revert to Dorothy Duncan. You probably think that my death in the near future is probable. That is true, but the future is nearer than you think. While making this confession to you I have, perhaps unnoticed, taken a deadly poison which will inevitably accomplish its end in a short time. I have made my confession, but I ask no forgiveness— I ask no pity or sympathy. But, Dorothy, remember I did it all for you. For you, darling—but I have failed."

With a last despairing look of love and longing at Dorothy, Crosby folded his arms on the table before him, and dropped his head upon them.

THE END

Other Resurrected Press Mysteries From Carolyn Wells

Resurrected Press Mysteries From Louis Tracy

The Albert Gate Mystery
Four men murdered and a fortune in diamonds belonging to the Turkish Sultan stolen, while the Foreign Office official in charge has gone missing. Was it a common jewelry theft or was it a case of international intrigue? This is the question that barrister detective Reginald Brett must solve.

The Bartlett Mystery
When Ronald Tower is murdered on his way to a bridge game on the yacht Sans Souci it at first appears a common crime. But as Rex Carshaw finds, a tragic case of mistaken identity leads to political scandal among the rich and powerful of New York.

The Strange Case of Mortimer Fenley
When the wealthy Mortimer Fenley is struck down by a shot from an express rifle on the steps of his mansion, detectives Winter and Furneaux of Scotland Yard must find the culprit. Was it the artist who claimed he was painting a picture at the time of the shot? The disaffected younger son? Or is there another suspect?

The Stowmarket Mystery
For five generations the Fergus-Hume family has been cursed. Each of the baronets has met a violent end. When the fifth baronet is found slain by a ceremonial Japanese dagger, suspicion falls on his cousin David. It falls to barrister detective Reginald Brett to prove his innocence and find the real murder in a case that spans two continents and as many centuries.

Visit www.resurrectedpress.com

Resurrected Press Mysteries by J. S. Fletcher

The Orange-Yellow Diamond

When an elderly pawnbroker is murdered in the London parish of Paddington, a young, down on his luck writer is accused of the crime. But then it's found the pawnbroker had had in his possession an extraordinary South African diamond worth over eighty-thousand pounds —a diamond that's now missing. It falls to Melky Rubenstein to unravel the mystery and prove the young man's innocence.

The Middle Temple Murder

When an elderly man's body is found on the steps of chambers in the Midde Temple, one of the Inns of Court, it falls to newspaperman Frank Spargo and Detective-Sergeant Rathbury to solve the crime. The murdered man, for indeed it was murder, was found with no money or identification on his person except for a piece of paper with the name and address of a young barrister. Who is the victim? Why was he killed? Who is the murderer?

Scarhaven Keep

Bassett Oliver, the famed actor, has gone missing. When Oliver fails to show for a rehearsal, aspiring playwright Richard Copplestone finds himself sent to the small village of Scarhaven on the northern coast of England to track down the actors movements. What he finds is mystery. Find the answers as Copplestone unravels the mystery of Scarhaven Keep.

Visit www.resurrectedpress.com

Resurrected Press Mysteries by Fergus Hume

The Green Mummy

Professor Braddock hoped to compare the burial practices of the Egyptians with those of the ancient Peruvians with his latest acquisition, the mummy of the last Inca, Caxas. But on arrival, the packing case proved to hold not the mummy, but the body of his assistant Sidney Bolton. It falls to Archie Hope to discover the murderer if he is to marry the professors step-daughter, Lucy Kendal. Who killed Bolton and where is the mummy? Was it the sea captain Hervey? The mysterious Don Pedro? Cockatoo the Polynesian servant? The professor, himself? And what has become of the emeralds? These are the questions that Hope must answer amongst the secrets of the past in The Green Mummy.

The Mystery of a Hansom Cab

"Truth is said to be stranger than fiction, and certainly the extraordinary murder which took place in Melbourne Friday morning goes a long way towards verifying that saying." Thus opens The Mystery of a Hansom Cab, the best selling mystery of the nineteenth century. When a man is found dead in a hansom cab one of Melbourne's leading citizens is accused of the murder. He pleads his innocence, yet refuses to give an alibi. It falls to a determined lawyer and an intrepid detective to find the truth, revealing long kept secrets along the way. Fergus Hume's first and perhaps most famous mystery... The Mystery Of A Hansom Cab.

Visit www.resurrectedpress.com

Resurrected Press Mysteries from the Dr. John Thorndyke Series

Dr. John Thorndyke Lecturer on Medical Jurisprudence and Forensic Medicine. Before Bones, before CSI, before Quincy, M.E– there was Dr. John Thorndyke solving the most baffling cases of Edwardian London using the latest tools of medical science. Read about his cases in:

The Eye of Osiris
John Bellingham, noted Egyptologist has vanished not once but twice in the same day. Now Dr, Thorndyke must unravel the tangled claims on his estate, solve the riddle of the missing man and find the "Eye of Osiris".

The Mystery of 31 New Inn
When Dr. Jervis is whisked away in a coach with no windows to an unknown location to treat a man in a coma from undivulged causes it is Dr. Thorndyke who must come up with the solution.

The Red Thumb Mark
The first of Dr. Thorndyke's cases finds him trying to prove the innocence of a young man accused of being a diamond thief despite the fact that his finger print was found at the scene of the crime.

John Thorndyke's Cases
More cases of medical mysteries as told by his trusted assistant Jervis, M.D. Eight stories of crime and deduction in Edwardian London.

Visit www.resurrectedpress.com

Resurrected Press Mysteries by John R. Watson & Arthur J. Rees

The Hampstead Mystery

High Court Justice Sir Horace Fewbanks found shot dead in his Hampstead home, a butler with a criminal past, a scorned lover and a hint of scandal. These are the elements of the Hampstead Mystery that Detective Inspector Chippenfield of Scotland Yard must unravel with the assistance of the ambitious Detective Rolfe. But will he be able to sort out the tangled threads of this case and arrest the culprit before he is upstaged by the celebrated gentleman detective Crewe. Follow the details of this amazing case at it plays out across Hampstead, London and Scotland until it reaches a stunning conclusion in the courts of the Old Bailey.

The Mystery of the Downs

When Harry Marsland was caught in a sudden down pour he sought shelter at Cliff Farm. Met at the door by a young woman clearly expecting someone else he is only too glad to get inside to wait out the storm. When they hear a noise upstairs in the deserted house they investigate only to discover the body of the farm's owner, Frank Lumsden, dead of a gunshot wound. Who then, killed Lumsden, and why? Who was the woman expecting and did she have any roll in the murder? These are the questions that private detective Crewe must answer in The Mystery of the Downs.

Visit www.resurrectedpress.com

Other Resurrected Press Mysteries

Mysteries on a Train

Before the Orient Express there was:

The Rome Express by Arthur Griffiths
A man is found dead in his first class sleeping compartment on the express from Rome to Paris. Who was his murderer? The Countess? The English General? His brother the clergy man? The maid who has disappeared? Is the French justice system up to solving the crime? Read about it in The Rome Express.

The Passenger from Calais by Arthur Griffiths
Colonel Basil Annesley finds he is the only passenger on the train from Calais to Lucerne. That is until a mysterious woman shows up at the last minute to book a compartment. Who is after her? What is her secret? Is she a criminal or a victim? Read about it in The Passenger from Calais

Visit us at www.resurrectedpress.com

About Resurrected Press

A division of Intrepid Ink, LLC, Resurrected Press is dedicated to bringing high quality, vintage books back into publication. See our entire catalogue and find out more at www.ResurrectedPress.com.

About Intrepid Ink, LLC

Intrepid Ink, LLC provides full publishing services to authors of fiction and non-fiction books, eBooks and websites. From editing to formatting, from publishing to marketing, Intrepid Ink gets your creative works into the hands of the people who want to read them. Find out more at www.IntrepidInk.com.